THE MISUNDERSTOOD ANGEL

(Branyrd the Angel Series Book 1)

J.E. SPINA

Thank you for respecting the hard work of this author.

ACKNOWLEDGEMENTS

A very special thank you to my wonderful beta readers, Patricia Bradley, Michelle Clement James, Michele Rolfe, John Spina and Frances Stewart for working tirelessly to read and review my work and for their helpful input. Their assistance is invaluable and appreciated.

DEDICATION

This paranormal fiction is dedicated to all who believe in angels around us. I think at the conclusion of this book those unbelievers may become believers too.

Thank you to my husband, John, for the beautiful cover, all the dinners he cooked that made it possible for me to continue to write, and for his support and encouragement. I love him dearly.

Table of Contents

PREFACE

This may appear to be a children's book or may be something for middle-graders. But don't let the title or the subject matter confuse you. It is for 18+.

There are things in this book that cannot be explained to young children. We all make mistakes but it is how we turn our lives around to correct them that matters. That is what the main protagonist in this story must do for not only herself, but for others too.

This is the first book in this series. This genre is different from what I have written in the past. I wanted to combine good and evil in a new way through the eyes of an angel named Branyrd.

There will be four books, possibly more, in this series. Each book will be a stand-alone story dealing in a new mission for the Angel, Branyrd.

Some may believe in angels on Earth while others are naysayers. I, for one, believe there is something out there that is helping us along our troubled paths and trying to steer us in the right direction. We all need help at one time or another in our lives.

Believe what you may, but after reading about this angel, you just may change your mind about believing. I hope it lightens your hearts and lifts your spirits.

Branyrd will better explain her role in this story. Here it is.

PROLOGUE

EARTH

The man drove as he was instructed to an alley which was vacant and filthy, evidenced by the garbage that was strewn about and the backs of buildings that were in dire need of repair. His boss told him that this was where his contact would be. He was instructed to wait there for the man with the red cap to appear.

There was a scuffle in the distance in the alley which alerted the driver this could be trouble. He saw three men coming his way after they pushed each other around and argued. The man in the front wore a red cap and was lanky and cocky in the way he carried himself. He was trying to appear in charge of this ragtag trio.

The driver could hear them arguing, "I don't have the money! Didn't you bring any? How are we going to get the stuff?"

Red Cap shushed the other man and kept on walking to the car that sat at the opposite end of the alley.

When the three men arrived next to the waiting car, the driver opened his window and looked out at them with a wary expression.

"Hey, do you have my stuff?" Red Cap inquired in a gruff voice filled with menace.

The two other men looked on, sniffled and rubbed noses which were already red. One was unsteady as he swayed TO and FRO.

Red Cap put his hand out to the driver and said, "I need my stuff."

The driver responded with a shake of his head, "Not until you give me the money."

"I...I don't have it. Please give it to me. I promise to pay you for it later this week."

"What do you think I am – stupid? Do you think my boss will accept your IOU?"

"Well, he knows me. He knows I will pay up. I always do," Red Cap insisted as he stared at the driver with glazed-over eyes.

The driver started up the car and prepared to drive away but was stopped by Red Cap as he held onto the window. The two fought as the driver tried to pry at Red Cap's fingers, banging repeatedly on Red Cap's knuckles. The car swerved and the driver almost lost control. After a few more attempts the driver succeeded in pulling Red Cap's fingers off the window. Red Cap's body flew through the air away from the speeding car and tumbled to the ground.

One of the other men reached inside his jacket and pulled out a gun, continually firing at the car as it raced away, nearly taking out the tires and back window.

Red Cap rolled over and groaned. He yelled, "What are you doing? You could have killed our only contact to get the stuff. What's wrong with you, stupid?"

The man with the gun put it back inside his pants and shrugged his shoulders. "I was only trying to scare him. I didn't even aim to hit him. I was trying to take out his tires then we could rob him of the smack and maybe beat him up a little."

Red Cap pulled himself up unsteadily and shook his head at the gun man. "Now what are we going to do? He will never come back here. I think your mother dropped you on your head too many times."

The man with the gun shrugged his shoulders, sniffled and hung his head.

The driver pushed the car to the limit evading the bullets as he heaved a sigh of relief. In his review mirror kept his eyes on the trio who still stood in the middle of the road now arguing back and forth.

The driver said out loud, "Hell, this is no way to make a living. I need to get a better job!"

CHAPTER ONE

HEAVEN

HE summoned Benedicto, one of his most trusted Guardian Angels, to come immediately.

Benedicto bowed to HIM and waited for instructions.

I want you to see something, Benedicto. HE replayed the scene that HE just witnessed on Earth for the angel.

"What does this mean, LORD?"

"It is the mission I had planned for Branyrd. That is, if she can get herself to the level of Angel First Class."

"Oh, yes, I see, LORD. Do you need my help getting her in line for this mission?"

"Yes, exactly, Benedicto. You are quite astute, angel. I think you will have a lot on your plate, but I trust you will not disappoint ME."

"Oh, I promise to do my best, LORD."

"And your best will be what I expect!"

In the meantime, I want you to keep your eyes on this man. His name is Nate. He is in trouble. What you saw is only the beginning. He also has a wife and young daughter. Your job is to guide Branyrd through this mission to help this family."

"Yes SIR!" Benedicto bowed and moved backward. When the angel looked up, HE was gone.

CHAPTER TWO

Heaven is a lonely place when you are a misfit and misunderstood. This is how Branyrd felt. Everywhere she looked she could see happy faces. Why wasn't she happy? What did she do wrong? Maybe HE could tell her. It was time to meet HIM if only St. Peter would allow her an audience. She sighed heavily and flew over to the house of the LORD. Of course, St. Peter was busy with all the incoming good souls and some not so acceptable souls which he had to redirect elsewhere.

All around were angels guarding the entrance to HIS Meeting Hall. They didn't even look at Branyrd as she waited patiently to get their attention. What was a pre-angel to do? How would she earn her wings if HE wouldn't even see her? What was she to do? She said a quiet prayer. Sometimes the quieter you are the more intently HE would listen to you. She closed her eyes and bowed her head to concentrate.

She opened her eyes when she felt a presence in front of her. She gasped in shock. It was *HIM*!

She couldn't find her voice or the words to even think about them so HE could read her mind. What was she to do? Oh no, she thought, HE might banish me forever to the unthinkable place!

"No, I would never do that, Branyrd! I listen to you and understand your plight. If you want to earn your place here in Heaven you must earn your way through good deeds."

"I...I...yes, I will do anything YOU...YOU ask of me, LORD. Whatever YOU ...YOU wish for me to do. I will do," she stuttered her words out.

HE smiled at her and placed HIS hands on her head as she bowed down to receive HIS grace.

Branyrd listened to HIS words and nodded as she thought over what HE had to say. She knew she would do whatever HE wanted her to do and earn her way as others had done before her.

"There is much you need to learn before you go on your first mission, Branyrd. I will be pairing you up with another, an Angel First Class, who will instruct you on what is expected of you before you are given a mission to help others on Earth."

"I am ready, LORD!" Branyrd exclaimed with excitement as her cloud sparkled in anticipation.

"You will go back to your cloud and wait there until I send along the Angel First Class. This angel will train you to complete a mission. It will take time to learn what you need to do. Even though time is not noted here in Heaven. Now, please go to your cloud and wait until further notice."

Branyrd nodded and bowed to the LORD as she backed away from HIM and proceeded to her cloud to wait for instructions about her training.

Bells tolled all over Heaven signaling the end of the meeting with the LORD. A special tinkling bell was heard every so often also when an angel received his/her First-Class level and a louder one signaling earning their wings. This was Branyrd's goal. She watched as HE elevated up toward the roof of the room and disappeared. All the angels kept looking up expecting HIM to come back down. They never tired of seeing HIM do this.

All the angels left the room except for some Guardian Angels First Class who stood guard outside the room 24-7. How they didn't get tired was never explained.

Only very special angels were ever considered to be Guardian Angels First Class. Branyrd knew she would never reach that honored level.

CHAPTER THREE

All Branyrd wanted was to be able to do what other angels do - help others on Earth. She was fascinated by the whisperings of bits and pieces of stories she heard from all the other angels who were given missions to help others. The Angels First Class all said they could not share everything with her or any other angels below them in Angel Status.

Branyrd was tired from waiting so long to be given a chance to prove herself. She tried not to think about all the times she had messed up. She knew she had to prove herself to HIM. She may not get another chance. She thought back to her mishaps while she kept a lookout for the Angel First Class for her training to begin.

Her mind roamed back over the day she had forgotten to report for her first meeting with HIM. The LORD had waited a long time for her to show up at his Meeting Room in the Great Hall. HE had finally sent two Angels First Class to bring her to HIM.

She shivered at the thought that she had been too busy having fun bouncing from cloud to cloud with her friends that she had forgotten her meeting with HIM. When the two Angels First Class found her bouncing around on the clouds, she had remembered the meeting.

"Oh no! I'm so sorry. I forgot all about the meeting with the LORD. I hope HE will forgive me!" she told the First Class Angels in a quivering voice.

The angels led the way for her and ignored her apology. They shook their heads and flew swiftly with her in tow to the meeting hall where the LORD was waiting for her. HE did not look pleased that she had forgotten their meeting.

Branyrd sputtered as she tried to explain away her ineptitude. "I…I…I'm so sorry, LORD! I didn't realize it was time for our meeting. I …I…forgot all about it, in fact. I was having fun with my fellow Angels Fourth Class."

"Hmm. I see! Branyrd, are you ready to move ahead to Angel Third Class? There is much for you to learn before you take your first mission."

"Yes, I…am ready, LORD. Whatever YOU need for me to do, I will do." Branyrd hung her cloud in shame, unable to meet the LORD'S eyes which were glowing with intensity.

HE waited for her to look up to explain what HE wanted her to do. "Since you did not come to our meeting in time, I will have to postpone your training until another time. There are other angels who are more serious about completing their training."

Branyrd jumped up in disappointment. "Oh no, LORD, I am so sorry. I am serious, I promise! What can I say to make YOU forgive me and let me begin my training?"

"There will be another time for you. In the meantime, Branyrd, you will think about this and work at being a better angel. You need more time to mature."

"But, LORD, I am grown up. I am not immature."

"You are excused, Branyrd. I will call you when I think you are ready for your training." The LORD turned away, disappearing into thin air leaving Branyrd feeling empty and alone.

It had felt like an eternity but finally, the day had come for Branyrd's training to begin. She couldn't wait. She was excited and anxious at the same time. She had no idea what she had to do. Most of her friends were Angels Fourth Class. Her best friend, Phera, was now an Angel First Class but she did not share any of her experiences about her training. Phera had told her that the LORD would not allow her to share anything that she had to do to rise to the next class.

Phera had shared a little about her mission on Earth where she helped a little boy come out of his shell and find a friend. She had told Branyrd of the wonders that were on the Earth that made it nothing like Heaven. There was much to learn and get used to once you arrive there.

Phera said, "I was nervous about meeting humans the first time and did not know how to interact with them. They were all different, some were easy to get along with while others were not nice at all."

Branyrd asked her friend many questions but still didn't understand what to do once she began her first mission there. Would she meet some people who were hard to get along with also? Would she like them? Would they like her?

Phera told her, "It's for you to find out on your first mission. The LORD does not want us to share what we do. I have told you more than I should have. Please don't share this with anyone else, Branyrd."

"Of course, Phera. My lips are sealed, I promise. Will HE downgrade you to an Angel Fourth Class again if HE finds out what you told me?"

"I don't know, but I don't want to take that chance. I have worked so hard to be where I am. You will find out what I mean when you begin your training too."

"Oh, Phera! I can't wait to begin. I am so excited. I just hope I won't mess things up like I always seem to do."

"You will be fine, Branyrd. I will say a few prayers for you."

"Thank you so much, Phera. I certainly need as many prayers as I can garner."

"Time for me to go. I have some new things to do…umm…I mean I…Oh, never mind. See you later, Branyrd."

"Okay, Phera. See you later." Branyrd hung her cloud. She felt left out of everything. Even Phera couldn't share simple things with her for fear of being demoted.

She flew over to another cloud where there were more Angels Fourth Class who, like her, were waiting for their training to begin.

"Hi everyone! Any news about when you will begin your training yet?"

The other angels exchanged nervous glances and flew away. They didn't even acknowledge Branyrd's question.

"What's going on? Why is everyone so secretive? We are all going through the same thing. How come you don't want to share anything with me?"

Oh, well! I guess it was the problems I caused them when I fell out of the cloud and pulled some of them with me. Oops! I know I should have been paying attention when I flew from one cloud to another. I am so clumsy. No wonder they call me a misfit. But I am just misunderstood. I am sure the LORD understands me. Branyrd sighed heavily and sat down on the large cloud to think.

While she was thinking about it, another one of her friends stopped by. Carmina was feeling sorry for Branyrd and came to cheer her up.

"Hi Branyrd. How are you doing?"

"Oh hi, Carmina. I'm doing okay, I guess. Why doesn't anyone want to talk to me?"

"I'm talking to you."

"Oh, right. You and Phera are the only Angels First Class who speak to me. All I want to know is what to expect when I do go to Earth on my first assignment. Will you share your experiences with me?"

"Well, we are told by HIM not to share everything. The only part I can share with you is how wonderful it feels. HE won't mind if I tell you I helped a little girl walk. That is all I can say. How and why, I can't share any of the other experiences I had while I was there. I'm sorry, Branyrd."

"That's okay. I guess I will have to do the same thing when I come back from my first time. I will be bursting, though, to share it all over Heaven. But I will have to keep it all to myself or otherwise burst out of my cloud."

"Ha-ha, you are so funny, Branyrd! Burst out of your cloud! That is so comical to imagine," Carmina laughed as her cloud changed into her human form.

"I can't wait to have a human form too like you and Phera do. That is so cool," Branyrd sighed.

"It only happens when an Angel First Class or higher experiences a human emotion like laughter, tears, sadness, etc. It is the way we blend in better when we go to Earth. Oops, I shouldn't have shared that with you, Branyrd. Sorry. I must be off. I have plenty to do. Talk to you soon."

CHAPTER FOUR

Branyrd received a message from the LORD, "Report to the cloud where all the other Angels Fourth Class are sitting."

When she arrived there, her fellow Angels Fourth Class looked up at her and were ready to fly to another cloud but were stopped by an Angel First Class who stood guard over the cloud and them.

The Angel First Class stayed in place and gestured to Branyrd to come forward. A message was received in her head from the angel stating, "You are to begin your training by watching over these Angels Fourth Class and instructing them to behave. Once you complete this assignment you will be given another. Do you understand?"

Branyrd nodded and then replied when she received a stern look from the Angel to acknowledge the message. "Oh, sorry. Yes, I understand, Angel First Class." She bowed and stood where the Angel instructed her in front of the other Angels Fourth Class.

"Hello, my fellow Angels Fourth Class."

These Angels Fourth Class stared at Branyrd and then went back to chattering away with one another. They completely ignored her when she tried to speak a few more times.

"Listen up. I am trying to talk to you. Don't you hear me?" Branyrd sighed in exasperation. *Was I like this with other angels? Do I ignore them too?*

She sat down on the cloud next to the angels and listened in on their conversations. They were all discussing what they would do when they became Angels First Class, just like she always did.

Branyrd leaned in closer and whispered, "I agree with you. I can't wait until I can become an Angel First Class and can go to Earth."

The other angels stopped talking and looked at her in surprise. One asked, "Are you an Angel Fourth Class too?"

Branyrd smiled and said, "Yes, but you are part of my training to move to Angel Third Class. Will you help me:"

They all looked at her with their clouds lopsided in shock. "What can we do for you?"

"I'm Branyrd. Listen up! I'm just like you. I want to become an Angel First Class one day too. You have to trust me. I'm only trying to do my job. I need your help."

"What do we have to do, Branyrd?" one curious angel asked as she stated her name, "I am Andora. What do you want me to do?"

"Hi, Andora. It's nice to meet you. You do look somewhat familiar. Did I knock you off a cloud in the past?"

"Umm, yes, I think you did. Maybe I shouldn't help you after all. Are you going to knock me off this cloud?" Andora asked with a nervous titter.

"No. I was just being infantile. I need to become more serious in order to please the LORD. I think we all have to do that in order to get elevated to the next level."

The rest of the angels were now listening to Branyrd as she explained how to behave so they would be noticed by the LORD.

One of the smaller angels with a dark cloud spoke up, "I have been an Angel Fourth Class for too long. I want to have a whiter cloud like the other Angels Third Class. Please tell me what I have to do, Branyrd."

Branyrd nodded and smiled inside her cloud which felt suddenly larger.

"Wow, look at your cloud, Branyrd! It is larger than it was a little while ago. What did you do to make it that way?" Andora asked in amazement.

"I don't know," Branyrd answered as she looked around to see that her cloud was indeed larger."

"It's also whiter than our clouds, Branyrd. That is not fair. You are an Angel Fourth Class too. Why is your cloud whiter than ours?"

Suddenly Branyrd heard a voice in her head that startled her. It was HIM. HE said, "Since you have proven your ability to control a situation and take charge, you are now elevated to an Angel Third Class, Branyrd. Congratulations! Keep up the good work!"

"Oh, my goodness! Did you hear that?" she looked at the other angels who were shaking their clouds and appearing perplexed.

"No, we didn't hear anything? Did you?" Andora turned to her fellow angels and they all shook their clouds negatively.

"I guess HE just spoke to me in my cloud then," Branyrd exclaimed in joy. *HE just spoke to me! I am an Angel Third Class! Yippee!* Branyrd jumped up and down on the cloud knocking over the other angels who were now quite upset.

"Oh, sorry about that. I was just excited to hear a message from the LORD!"

"HE spoke to you just now?" another angel asked, in confusion.

"Yes, HE did! I can't believe it! HE just elevated me to Angel Third Class!" Branyrd said, beaming.

"Wow! That was fast. What did you do to gain that level? Please tell us. We want to be Angels Third Class too," they all yelled out to her.

"I don't know. But whatever it is I better keep doing it," Branyrd smiled and nodded at the angels.

"Well, when you figure it out, please let us know," Andora stated, clearly disgruntled as she exchanged nods with her fellow angels. Their clouds moved up and down with their motions displaying their indignation.

CHAPTER FIVE

Branyrd, now Angel Third Class, couldn't believe her luck was changing. She had no idea what she had done to earn this promotion or elevation. She would have to be careful not to mess this up and lose it.

The other angels did say that her cloud was larger and whiter than theirs. Maybe that is because she was watching her language now. She can't even think about anything that would make HIM demote her. Maybe that is why she has not been promoted in the past.

She always had some four-letter words in her head when she had gotten angry with other angels. Now she couldn't do that. Oh boy, just saying this had her thinking of them now.

Stop it now, Branyrd whispered to herself. *You must clear up your act or you will never be promoted to the next level. You will always be a misfit forever and ever.*

Before Branyrd could contain her thoughts, she heard HIS voice in her head warning her to behave. Just as HE was moving out of her head, she thought she heard a chuckle.

What was that? Branyrd whispered. Did she hear correctly? Did the LORD just giggle in her head?

She had often heard HE had a sense of humor. Maybe that's true. Branyrd giggled just thinking about it.

Branyrd went back to traveling from cloud to cloud and now mingling with the other Angels Third Class. They looked at her and smiled, or at least their clouds looked happy to see her. She hadn't learned how to show emotion other than when she was angry and her cloud got dark and menacing. It even frightened her.

There was a lot of whispering as she came closer to the group who were huddling together. They quieted down once they saw her approach.

"Hello. I am Branyrd, Angel Third Class." She edged closer as she introduced herself.

The other Angels Third Class stopped whispering and looked at her. "Hello," one angel said and bowed her cloud up and down at Branyrd. "Nice to meet you, Branyrd."

"It's nice to meet you too. I just got my promotion to Angel Third Class which was quite a surprise. I didn't expect it at all since I can never do anything right in HIS EYES. I don't feel very steady right now."

"Um, yes, we see that. Your cloud keeps bouncing up and down. Are you all right, Branyrd?" another Angel Third Class enquired as she turned her cloud upside down to look at Branyrd.

"Yes, I am quite content and damn happy! Holy shit! Oops again! Sorry, I didn't mean to say that. I forgot my manners. It was in my head and just came out. I have to learn to curb the vulgarity or HE may change HIS mind about my promotion."

"Most definitely," one Angel Third Class responded with a snicker. "My name is Estella. It is refreshing to meet you, Branyrd. I have never met any angel like you. You are not afraid to share your feelings even if you misspoke just now."

"Ha, ha, you could say that. I am different. I've been told that all my angel life. I hope HE thinks I misspoke just now too." Branyrd giggled and caused all the other angels to giggle too. Their clouds displayed their emotions by floating up and down like Branyrd's.

The LORD sent two Angels First Class to the cloud to check on Branyrd and the other angels Third Class. HE didn't like what he was hearing and was fearful Branyrd was instigating a change in the other angels with her language. HE had to do something to stop her from using it or HE would have to demote her back to fourth class.

The Angels Third Class were so busy giggling and chatting away like old friends that they did not see the two stern-looking Angels First Class standing at the edge of the cloud staring in their direction.

Branyrd felt something in the air and turned around abruptly and saw the two Angels First class. She exclaimed before she could stop herself, "What the hell?"

The two angels shook their heads at her and pointed their hands in her direction pulling her toward them. Branyrd found herself in their clutches and being dragged away through the air back to the LORD's Meeting Room once again.

Branyrd looked back at the shocked clouds who shook in fear at Branyrd's situation and what her fate could be.

Back at the immense Meeting Room of the LORD. HE looked down on Branyrd with lightning coming out of HIS eyes. This light was too bright for Branyrd to look at. She closed her cloud and folded it together to keep the brightness away.

HE kept looking at her and sending his thoughts to her as HE shook HIS head.

"What were you thinking, Branyrd? Did you not like being an Angel Third Class today? It hasn't been that long since you received this promotion."

Branyrd unfolded her cloud and spread it out to reply to the LORD. "I am so terribly sorry, dear LORD, for my behavior. I don't know what happens to me. I can't seem to keep those words out of my cloud. I feel dirty now and need to clean my cloud. Please, please forgive me!" Branyrd bowed as low as she could go with her cloud and flattened it out at the feet of the LORD.

HE looked down at Branyrd and cleared HIS throat before answering. HE did this again but this time HE actually guffawed a little, or so it sounded like a guffaw.

Branyrd waited for the LORD to continue whatever HE was trying to say to her. She was confused about HIS odd behavior. It wasn't like HIM to act like this. HE appeared to be at a loss for words.

She didn't dare move for fear of insulting HIM. She let her cloud lay flat on the ground instead of floating a little above the floor. She waited some more and didn't look up. Her cloud was trembling now and she was afraid she would shed water all over the floor from her sweating.

"Branyrd, look up at ME!"

"Yes, LORD." Branyrd lifted her cloud off the floor and elevated it to look up to the LORD who was nearly at the rafters of the room. HE was glowing and HIS arms were spread toward her.

She was definitely sweating now. There was a puddle growing under her cloud. She tried to keep the unspoken forbidden words out of her head as she concentrated on only good thoughts.

"What are you thinking now, Branyrd?" HE asked her.

"I...I...don't know, LORD. I mean...I don't mean what is in my head at the moment. Please forgive me."

"Yes, I see there are some things there that should be erased right now. Let ME erase them for you." HE waved HIS hands over her cloud and it became clean once again.

"Thank you, LORD. That feels much better," Branyrd sighed and shivered as she tried to soak up the puddle under her.

"Don't worry about that, Branyrd. My Angels First Class will take care of that. Now I want to see and hear that you are behaving yourself. I need you for some missions that are coming up. These missions need you to earn your Wings to First Class. I will give you a bigger assignment when you reach Angel Second Class though to get you prepared for tougher assignments."

"Oh, yes, LORD! I can't wait to go on my first mission. I will do all I can to make YOU proud of me and clean up my language, once and for all."

"That is good to hear, Branyrd. Now, get back to work rehabilitating the other angels lower than you. Also, do not visit with the other Angels Third Class today. I plan on working with them myself to erase what you did."

"Sorry about that, LORD. I promise not to visit them today. But can I visit them tomorrow?"

Branyrd did not get an answer but did receive a gust of hot wind that blew her back to the cloud on which HE wanted her to begin work.

CHAPTER SIX

Branyrd worked tirelessly with her Angels Fourth Class recruits all day long even if there was no time in Heaven. No clocks or even days to count. It was like one long day never-ending. She didn't dare even look toward the cloud with her fellow Angels Third Class for fear that HE would demote her.

She also knew there were two Angels First Class close by at all times keeping a watchful eye over her. She didn't want to disappoint HIM in any way. HE may change HIS mind about giving her a mission once she reached her First-Class status. That's if she ever did! She sighed heavily and instructed the Angels Fourth Class to listen up.

Branyrd finally got their attention once again to explain what they needed to do to receive a promotion as she did. She still didn't know what she had done to gain HIS trust after all she had done in the past, especially with her language.

She didn't understand where this bad language came from. She mused over it as the angels stood in front of her watching her cloud change color from white to gray and back again.

Branyrd shook her cloud to clear it and looked at the recruits. She rippled her cloud trying to show some emotion to them, to no avail. She wasn't, after all, at that level to show any kind of emotion except her anger or disappointment in shades of gray or nearly black.

The Angels Fourth Class began to act up again when Branyrd appeared to be in her own world and not receptive to them or their errant behavior. Branyrd woke up from her stupor and noticed the Angels Fourth Class were bouncing around and hanging from one cloud to another.

She shouted at them, "Stop that right now!" They were so surprised at her sudden yelling that they slipped and fell to the cloud below them, which was the one Branyrd was supposed to stay away from. The Angels Third Class looked up at her and the mischievous Angels Fourth Class and showed their discontent in shades of dark gray.

Branyrd quickly pulled the Angels Fourth Class back up onto the cloud and didn't look at the other Angels Third Class. She was embarrassed to say the least. She had looked incompetent. How was she going to explain this blooper to HIM?

The rowdy Angels Fourth Class laughed and cavorted once again as Branyrd tried in vain to get them to listen. She clapped her cloud together causing a loud boom to get their attention.

All Angels Fourth Class looked at her and aligned their clouds close together as if standing to attention like soldiers. Branyrd was quite pleased that this tactic worked on them.

"Well, it's about time I got your attention, Angels Fourth Class. If you want to stay at Fourth Class status forever just keep up this behavior. HE notices everything, remember that."

Branyrd waved her cloud menacingly at them to make her point. They shook, in return, with fear and their clouds drooped heavily. The clouds filled with perspiration that began to drip onto the floor of the cloud where they stood and threatened to pour over onto the other clouds below.

"What are you doing, Angels Fourth Class? Are you trying to get all of us demoted to the place we shall not name?"

One Angel Fourth Class stepped forward and bent her cloud in a bow. "We are really sorry, Branyrd, Angel Third Class. What can we do to make up for our awful behavior?"

"Well, first of all you need to soak up that puddle beneath you so it won't drip down to the other clouds. The LORD has not commanded us to rain down on the Earth today. You need to save your moisture for when it is needed."

The angels all nodded their clouds up and down in agreement and began to soak up the moisture they had expelled below and around them.

"Nice work, Angels Fourth Class. Now let's discuss what you should do to improve your behavior," Branyrd floated above them.

The Angels Fourth Class gawked and oohed and aahed at the sight of Branyrd as she hovered over them. They bowed down to her and spoke out loud, "Look at your cloud, Branyrd, Angel Third Class! It is getting brighter and bigger and spreading out in all directions!"

"What? What is happening to me?" Branyrd shivered as she felt her cloud pulling her out this way and that. It felt bigger and looked whiter as she watched it continue to become more brilliant.

The Angels Fourth Class dropped to the cloud base and shook in fear as they looked not only at Branyrd but now also at the LORD who hovered above Branyrd causing her cloud to brighten even more.

"Branyrd! Look up at ME!" the LORD commanded.

Branyrd shivered with fear but managed to look above her and meet the LORD's brilliant eyes. "What did I do, LORD? Are you unhappy with me again? Please forgive me for whatever you find displeasing."

"No, I am not displeased with you, Branyrd, Angel Second Class. You are doing a wonderful job. Just what I expected from you. You have proven you can handle unruly subjects in an efficient and timely manner; therefore, you have earned another level. Continue on with your work with these recruits."

Before Branyrd could respond HE was gone. She looked around and noticed the recruits were whiter too but not as white as her cloud. She nodded to them and they responded with a sweep of their clouds.

"Did you hear what HE said to you, Branyrd? HE called you Branyrd, Second Class Angel!" one angel exclaimed.

"What? Did HE really say that? I thought I had imagined it! Am I truly an Angel Second Class now?" Branyrd couldn't contain her joy and jumped up and flew around the other angels.

"Yes, I think that is what HE said," another angel responded.

Branyrd couldn't believe it! She had received another promotion all in one sequence or whatever it was! It certainly felt like it was an eternity if she could measure such things in Heaven. Wow! She was so happy that she twirled around and around making the other angels dizzy. She felt as light as the air around her.

She sighed, content and surprised at this new development. She couldn't wait to share the news. But would HE want her to tell anyone? HE didn't want her to go to the other angels Third Class. They would be shocked to hear her news. Should she have asked HIM what she could do?

Before she could ponder this further, Branyrd heard HIS voice in her head instructing her to go to another cloud to work with some other recruits. "Branyrd, go to the ninth cloud now and straighten out the unruly angels who are causing havoc there. Once you complete this assignment, I will contact you for your next job."

"Yes, LORD. I obey. I am on my way there now."

When she arrived, the cloud was shaking and moving all over making it difficult for her to stand on it. There were too many Angels Fourth Class misbehaving to count. They were pulling and pushing each other and banging their clouds together to make a booming sound as she had done before. She could hear their laughter vibrating throughout the cloud base.

Now what am I going to do with these foolish angels? Does HE think I am up to this task? How am I going to straighten them out?

Branyrd floated above the errant angels and blew warm air around them. She managed to push them all together in a line of clouds that looked unhappy but at least were quiet for the time being.

CHAPTER SEVEN

Branyrd shook her cloud back and forth sending a spray of water over the heads of the Angels Fourth Class causing them to stop what they were doing.

They looked up at her large white cloud that hovered over them and sprinkled water that hit them like icicles. They shivered in fear.

Branyrd spoke loud and clear, "What do you think you are doing, Angels Fourth Class? Do you think you will ever gain HIS favor by acting this way?"

The Angels Fourth Class shook their clouds and caused a rumbling sound since they were so close together.

"I hope this means you understand what I am saying?" Branyrd exclaimed sternly.

One Angel answered in a shaky voice, "Yes, Angel Second Class, we understand. Are you going to expel us to HIM?"

"No, I cannot do that. I would have to be an Angel First Class to do that. But I can report your horrible behavior to HIM."

"We are truly sorry, Angel Second Class. Please do not report us."

Branyrd looked down upon one cloud which was smaller than the rest. It appeared to be ready to disappear in fright.

"What is your name, Angel Fourth Class with the little cloud?"

"Oh, please don't report me. I am so sorry, Angel Second Class."

"I will not report you. Please tell me your name. You do have a given name, don't you?" Branyrd softened her voice to calm the small angel.

"I…I am Marena. I have always been smaller than the other angels. I can't help that."

"Nice to meet you, Marena. You do not have to explain your size to me. I was always small too when I was at your status. The LORD makes us grow with each class we reach. Once you are an Angel First Class you will be just as large as the other angels, if not bigger."

"Really? I will be as big as all of these other angels one day."

Branyrd nodded, bouncing her cloud up and down.

The other Angels Fourth Class made a razzing sound in disbelief at this statement by Marena.

Branyrd turned her attention to these angels and her cloud showed her anger as it turned black.

"What do you think you are doing by making that sound, Angels Fourth Class?"

The guilty angels bowed down and shuddered at Branyrd's words. They were too frightened to answer.

Marena watched as her fellow Angels Fourth Class were now smaller than she. She looked around and saw her cloud had grown and become whiter than theirs.

The LORD'S voice was heard all around them. "You Angels Fourth Class are not going to the next level because of your unkind behavior to one of your own. You are to stay here on this cloud and learn how to behave with the next Angel Third Class who will be here to teach you good behavior. Marena, you have earned your next step to Angel Third Class. Congratulations! You will stay here to train these errant Angels Fourth Class until otherwise given another assignment."

Marena humbly bowed down and exclaimed, "Thank you, LORD! I am truly grateful!"

The LORD smiled down on Marena and directed his next words to Branyrd, "As for you, Branyrd, you have shown true diligence in dealing with fellow angels and earned their respect by your inspiring behavior. You are now an Angel First Class. I expect to see you in my Meeting Room immediately."

Branyrd jumped up and down, joining Marena in a happy cloud dance. They made circles around the unhappy Angels Fourth Class who were gray and curled up together weeping.

They all looked up to see the LORD had disappeared as always so quickly that they hadn't noticed when.

CHAPTER EIGHT

Branyrd flew directly to the LORD'S Meeting Room where all the Angels First Class were standing around in formation.

Above her head she felt a presence and a cool breeze that blew throughout her cloud changing it in a way she never imagined.

She looked down to see that she now had feet and a whole body which was clothed in a brilliant white cloak. On her back was a long sword in a scabbard which had no weight but glistened as she ran her hands over it.

Branyrd looked around and saw all the Angels First Class smiling at her and bowing as the LORD came down in front of her and raised HIS hands over her to bless her and prepare her for what was coming next. A bell sounded reverberating across Heaven signaling another angel made Angel First Class and then a second louder one rang announcing that Branyrd now had wings.

Branyrd smiled back at her fellow Angels and bowed to HIM. She tried to speak but found she had no voice. She felt something sweeping around her and saw her wings, a brilliant white in color with a feathery, soft and unbelievably light texture. They appear to glisten and float in the air around her. She could feel herself being lifted up to meet HIS eyes.

HE answered her questions that were running through her head in confusion.

"Yes, you are now an Angel First Class, Branyrd. I have given you a body so you can prepare to go to Earth to perform your first mission. Your wings will not be visible to humans but only be there when you are back in HEAVEN."

Branyrd nodded and cleared her throat and tried again to speak. "I…um…," she coughed and coughed.

"Yes, I have given you a new voice to go with your new body, Branyrd. You must get used to using it. You are no longer a cloud and must speak through your mouth and not through the many spaces in your cloud."

Branyrd tried once again. "I…I can speak, LORD. It does feel funny to speak out of a mouth instead of a cloud which has many mouths, I guess. What do you wish for me to do, LORD?"

The LORD wasn't there in front of her but above her once again. HE spoke into her head and raised HIS hands over her as HE said, "Branyrd, I now christen you an Angel First

Class. You are to go to Earth. I will send messages to your brain and you will decipher what you must do when you reach Earth."

"But, LORD, what am I to do there? Where must I go?"

"You need not worry, Branyrd. I will send another more experienced Angel First Class, your Guardian Angel, with you to get you settled. Once you understand your mission, you must proceed to complete it in a timely fashion. Each day, and there are hours in a day on Earth, you must report to me whatever you have accomplished. If you have any problems at all, you must contact the Angel First Class, who will be your advisor on Earth. He will be close by to aid you if you have any problems. He cannot do the job for you though. He can only be your counsel. Do you understand, Branyrd?"

Branyrd bowed and answered, "Yes, my LORD. I understand. I am frightened of the unknown at the moment. But I guess I will learn as I go."

"Yes, I expect you are a little unsure of yourself right now. Once you begin your mission, it will all come to you easily enough. I will be here if you need ME also. I am only a thought away."

"Yes, I appreciate that LORD. I'm sure I will need YOU."

"Be on your way, now, Branyrd, Angel First Class. May your mission be successful and happy."

"Thank you, LORD, for this opportunity to shine and show you I am worthy."

Branyrd looked around but HE was gone. Standing in front of her was the largest Angel First Class she had ever encountered. He stood at least eight feet tall next to her five and a half feet. She felt miniscule in comparison. Before she could ask him a question, he spoke in her head.

"Branyrd, Angel First Class, I am Guardian Angel, Benedicto, Angel First Class on High. I will bring you to Earth and be there if you need guidance as the LORD has instructed you already. Are you ready to begin your first mission?"

"Yes, I am, Benedicto, Angel First Class on High. I am honored to meet one whose name means 'blessed.'"

There was a whirring sound and the clouds were swirling around and opening to a land beyond – Earth.

Branyrd felt herself falling through the clouds and down onto this land that was utterly different from Heaven but beautiful in a new way. There were so many colors in front of her like a rainbow – red, orange, yellow, green, blue, indigo and violet. The land was green and stood out against the azure blue of the sky. There were tall green things – trees and beautiful flowers all around. It all took her breath away. She could hear Benedicto's voice in her head as she questioned him about everything she saw.

Benedicto smiled at Branyrd as he observed her shock at her first glance of Earth. He had felt similar feelings of incredulity. No place could be as beautiful as Heaven but Earth had a different quality of beauty at first glance. He knew her view of this planet would soon change once she got close and saw what it really looked like. He only hoped she would be able to complete her mission after she learned more about this new place called Earth. It wasn't all it seemed.

The two angels were outfitted on the way down with the proper clothes to fit into their surroundings. Benedicto now stood at an average height of six feet tall, wore jeans with holes at his knees and a well washed t-shirt and dark blue sneakers. The Guardian Angel could still appear to others at his full height of over eight feet tall if he wanted to.

Branyrd looked down at her own outfit and gasped. She no longer was dressed all in white with a scabbard and incredible wings but now had a smaller body of just over five feet tall. She felt healthy and strong. She breathed deeply through her nose and giggled when the air tickled her hand as it expelled out of this new orifice. She had on a lighter shade of jeans than Benedicto, a pink t-shirt and purple sneakers with sparkles.

They landed softly on a paved way, and blended into the crowds around them who were unaware of their entrance. As they walked along Branyrd saw a logo, White Stag Gang, spray-painted on a wall. Whatever did that mean? She looked at Benedicto and sent a question to his mind.

"What does White Stag Gang mean?"

"We will soon find out, Branyrd. Be patient. We must find a room for you to stay while you are here. There is someone you must meet to begin your mission. Here we are, the YWCA. This is a safe place for you."

CHAPTER NINE

A man buzzed them into the building after they identified themselves as looking for a room. Branyrd looked around at the foyer of this place called the YWCA. It was wide open with plenty of couches, chairs and a TV in one corner and card tables in the other where several women sat playing games of some sort.

She had never seen a TV before. It was supposed to have pictures on it that moved, she had heard. Benedicto had tried to fill her in on some of the things that she would encounter and the TV was one of them. She was fascinated and couldn't wait to see it up close. She gazed at the pictures that were on the screen now and looked on in awe. Benedicto had to pull her away from it.

Branyrd wondered what the name YWCA meant but didn't want to sound stupid to ask in front of the man who stood behind a high counter observing them.

Benedicto guided Branyrd forward as he spoke with the man. "I need a room for this young lady for two weeks, maybe more. Do you have anything available, sir?"

"Yes, I have just the room for her. What about you, sir? This place is only for women. Did you know that?"

"Oh no, I am just passing through and helping my friend to find a place to stay. I have my own accommodations, thank you."

The tall man, older and balding with kind brown eyes, looked down at Branyrd and smiled. She couldn't help but smile back at him.

"Do you have any luggage with you, miss? I can have someone help you carry it upstairs. Our elevator is, unfortunately, not working at the moment which happens too often, in my opinion," he said with an exasperated sigh.

Branyrd looked up at Benedicto waiting for him to say something to the man. She didn't have any luggage.

"No problem, sir. I will assist my friend to her room. What floor and number?" Benedicto asked.

Picking up a key off a hook behind him and handing it to Branyrd, the man answered, "Third floor, room 305 to the right of the stairs. You can help the young lady to her room but you cannot stay."

"Thank you, sir. I understand. I will be leaving shortly after I escort the lady to her room," Benedicto turned to Branyrd and said, "This way, Branyrd. I will help you with your luggage."

Branyrd looked at her Guardian Angel with a quizzical expression wrinkling her brow. She whispered, "What luggage, Benedicto?"

Bending down to lift up a small blue suitcase, Benedicto stated with a wink, "This suitcase, Branyrd."

She blinked and rubbed her eyes but the blue suitcase was still there. Now, where did that come from and what was in it?

Benedicto led the way for a puzzled fellow angel who could not stop shaking her head in disbelief.

When they reached room 305 Benedicto pointed to the keyhole as he waited for Branyrd to understand what to do. "Put the key into the hole and turn it, Branyrd. The door will open for you."

She did as he instructed and jumped back as the door swung in. She stepped inside and looked around. It was a small room with one window, a twin size bed against the wall next to the window, a night stand with a lamp, a chest of drawers, a desk with a chair and a little closet.

Benedicto explained what everything was and how to use them. "There is a bathroom where you relieve yourself. This is something new to you since you have never done that before. You will share it with three other rooms. You must take your turn."

Branyrd was even more confused now. What in the world was a bathroom? She opened the door and walked down the hall to look at it with Benedicto close behind.

She peeked inside the small room that held a deep bathtub, a toilet and a sink with towel racks. Benedicto explained it all to her and smiled. "I know it is strange, but you will get used to it all. You use the toilet paper to clean yourself after voiding and whatever else comes out of you." He tried to hold back a laugh when he saw the shocked expression on this newest Angel First Class's face. He couldn't contain it any longer and let out a deep and robust laugh.

"What is so funny, Benedicto? I don't understand any of this? I thought I was an angel and not a human. What have you done to me?"

He put a serious expression on his face and stated in a calm voice, "I am only kidding you, Branyrd. You do not have to worry about any of this. But you must act normal at all costs. Each day you have to go to this room even if you do not have to use it. Others will see you go in and not think of you as inhuman that way. Try to act like everyone around you so as not to cause others to be alarmed. They do not know you are an angel."

Branyrd tried not to think of some choice words to say to her Guardian Angel but controlled herself for fear of HIM reading her mind. Instead, she sighed loudly and avoided meeting Benedicto's eyes.

"Do you understand all this, Branyrd? Do you have any questions?"

"Yes, what is in the suitcase? What do I do in this room?"

"The suitcase is just for the clerk to see. It is really not even here. If you look around, you will see it is gone. There are changes of clothes for you in the drawers and closet. You must change each day. When you take an outfit out of one drawer another will take its place. You will never run out of clothes and will not have to wash them either. When you are ready to leave here the suitcase will appear once again. As for this room, this is where you will sleep or stay until HE instructs you to go somewhere to begin your mission."

"Okay. What do I do while I wait for HIS instructions?"

"Well, you could go downstairs and meet the other women who are staying here. You could play cards or other games with them. I'm sure they would teach you."

"But when can I begin my mission? Will I have to wait very long, Benedicto?"

"That I cannot say. It is for HIM to say, not me. I am only here at HIS request to be your guardian and watch over you to ensure you do not get into any kind of trouble."

"Hmm, I see. Well, what are you going to do in the mean...?"

Before Branyrd could finish her sentence, Benedicto had disappeared.

"Now where did he go? What am I supposed to do? I don't know if I am going to like this."

CHAPTER TEN

Branyrd looked around the room at everything. She opened the closet which was full of clothes, tops, jackets and pants. Next, she opened the drawers of the chest which were also full of smaller articles of clothing. She looked inside the nightstand drawer and saw a Bible. At least she would have something to read, she thought. Even though these words were not HIS.

She tested out the bed by bouncing up and down on it. It wasn't nearly as soft as her cloud in Heaven. But if she wanted, she could lay down like she did on her cloud and think, sing or just hum.

She found herself humming along with a tune she suddenly heard in the hall. She looked outside her room and saw a woman sweeping the floor and singing a song. She had something hanging out of her ears that led to another object tucked into her clothes.

Branyrd walked out of her room and called out to the woman. The woman did not turn around at her voice but continued to sing a pleasant song in a lovely voice. It was angelic in nature, Branyrd thought. Maybe she is an angel too.

The thought of having another angel here brightened Branyrd's spirits a little. She walked closer to the woman and tapped her on the shoulder. The woman cried out in alarm and nearly fell over.

"Oh, I am so sorry. Are you all right? I didn't mean to frighten you. I am Branyrd. I just moved in. I may be staying for a couple of weeks or so. What's your name?"

"I'm okay. I didn't hear you. I was listening to music on my phone. Sorry. I'm Maggie. I've been here for a month now. I had to get aw…"

"Hi Maggie. What did you have to get away from? I figured that is what your last word was going to be. Right?"

"Umm, well. I'm busy now. I have to finish sweeping up this floor and move onto the other floors. There are seven floors to clean. I have to do this to pay my rent since I don't have any money."

"Oh. I'm sorry to hear that. I don't have…Oh, never mind. That is not important."

"What isn't important, Branyrd? Where do you come from? Your voice sounds like it has an accent from somewhere. I can't place it."

"Well, that is because I am not from around here." Branyrd stopped herself from revealing any more.

"Excuse me, Branyrd. I must finish up so I can go pick up my daughter from school."

"You have a daughter? How nice. Can I meet her sometime?"

"Well, I guess so since you are staying here for a while."

Branyrd smiled and excused herself. "Sorry to keep you from your work, Maggie. See you again soon and your daughter too."

The Angel First Class walked downstairs to see who else she could meet. It was better than staying in her room all alone.

At the bottom of the stairs, she saw a large group of women playing games at the few tables. She went over to the first group and leaned in to see what they were doing.

One woman turned to look at her and pushed her away. "What do you think you are doing looking at my cards. Are you trying to help someone cheat me?"

"What? Oh, no. I was just curious to see what you were playing. I never played cards before. Can you teach me how to play?"

The four women exchanged confused looks and then continued on with their game, ignoring Branyrd.

Branyrd moved over behind a second woman and looked at her cards. The woman put her cards down and turned to the angel. "Now what are you doing? Don't you understand we are trying to play cards? Go away and bother someone else."

The angel bowed her head and went over to the second table to see what the other women were playing. They had cubes and were throwing them down and clapping their hands. It looked like fun. She leaned over to watch them.

One woman looked up at her and exclaimed, "Get away from here. We do not have room for you. Go play with the other women at that table." She pointed at the next table a few feet away.

Branyrd went to the next table. She watched from further away this time as the four women had something flat and colorful on the table with many little objects sitting on different areas. They threw some more cubes with dots on them across the table and then moved little items around the flat thing. They exchanged paper and cheered.

One woman who had just received the paper objects turned around and looked at her. "Hi. Do you want to play Monopoly?"

"Monopoly? What is that?"

"Oh my," another woman exclaimed in surprise. "You never played Monopoly before?"

"Umm, no. Sorry. I never played any of these games before. I don't come from around here. Where I come from, we don't have games like this."

"Where is that?" another woman asked.

"Well, it is called Hea…. I mean it is called Haven."

"Haven? I think I heard of that. It's in Florida, right?"

Branyrd didn't know where Florida was but just nodded.

The kind woman who first spoke to her pulled up another chair for Branyrd to sit down and join them. She said, "I am Greta. What is your name?"

"I am Branyrd. Nice to meet you, Greta. Can you teach me how to play Monopoly?"

"Yes, of course."

The other women nodded and smiled at Branyrd making her feel welcome unlike the other two tables of unfriendly women.

Once Branyrd understood the premise of the game they played for over an hour and a half when a bell was heard. The women jumped up and headed to another room.

Greta pulled Branyrd up and told her, "It's time for lunch. Did you pay for a lunch every day?"

"I don't know. My friend got me this room. He did not tell me about food."

Greta looked at Branyrd. "Don't you eat?"

"I guess I can." Branyrd shrugged her shoulders and followed Greta to the dining room where there was a long table with covered containers that emitted heat and steam.

She got in line behind Greta and several other women and observed what they did before it was her turn. She watched them as they lifted up the containers and used a large object to scoop out whatever was in there.

Branyrd looked at the contents of one container that had dark colored substances with large things floating in it. Her stomach turned. She couldn't reach out to take any.

Greta enquired, "Can I help you, Branyrd? Have you had beef stew before? How about salad? Take a roll too."

Before she knew it Greta had filled her plate and was guiding her to a table to sit down and eat with her friends.

"Hey, everyone, this is Branyrd. She just moved here from Florida."

Everyone responded with a "Hi, Branyrd. Nice to meet you. Welcome to Glaser."

"Glaser?"

"Yes, this is Glaser, Massachusetts."

The other women frowned and looked at each other, shrugged their shoulders and continued eating.

"Oh, yes. I forgot. Sorry about that," Branyrd said, trying to cover up her blooper. She remembered what Benedicto had told her about blending in and not appearing different.

Branyrd managed to eat a little and then excused herself. She told them, "Sorry I have to use the bathroom."

The women nodded and Branyrd made her escape, for she really had to use the bathroom.

Once back in her room, Branyrd summoned Benedicto.

"What am I supposed to do now?"

"Ah, I see you have made some friends, Branyrd. That is wonderful! You are part of the group now and no one will suspect you are not like them."

"You didn't tell me I had to eat this stuff! It was awful! I spit it out in the toilet. I really had to use it this time. Do I have to eat this stuff every day?"

"No, I will leave a sandwich in your room for you. You don't have to eat it though. Just scrunch it up and throw it away in the large barrel in the dining room when you are done with it. No one has to know that you didn't eat some of it."

"Thank you, Benedicto. While you are here, can you tell me when I will begin my mission?"

"Well, as a matter of fact your mission has already begun."

"What?"

CHAPTER ELEVEN

Branyrd shook her head and said, "No it hasn't! I haven't done anything yet."

"Oh, but you have. You have met your mission already," Benedicto insisted.

"Who? Greta?"

"No. The first person you recently met is your mission."

"Maggie? What do I have to do for her?"

"You will see soon enough. Now rest on the bed. You may not sleep but you will have time to think about this. HE will let you know what you must do."

"Okay, but I don't understand, Benedicto."

Branyrd looked around her as she lay on the bed but as usual her Guardian Angel had once again disappeared.

She sighed and closed her eyes to visualize Heaven. She missed it and all her fellow angels. Earth wasn't much fun even though she did meet some nice ladies and learned how to play Monopoly.

She couldn't wait to find out what her mission was. She knew who she would be helping, but what did Maggie need from her?

She was busy with her head in Heaven when she heard a knock on her door. She looked at the clock on her nightstand. It was already 7:30 am. She must have fallen asleep. She had never done that before.

She tiptoed to the door and opened it a crack. A little girl stood there with tears in her eyes. "Can you help me?"

Branyrd welcomed the little girl into her room and told her to sit down on the chair next to the desk.

"What is your name? What's wrong, little one? Why are you crying?"

"I'm Annie. My mother is sick. She is laying down but I can't wake her up."

"Where is your mother's room. Take me there so I can help her."

Annie led the angel to the room next door. She opened up the door and pointed to her mother in the twin bed next to the wall.

Branyrd looked down on the woman who appeared to be sleeping. She shook the woman's shoulder and tapped her on the arm, to no avail. She turned the woman over to see her face.

She was shocked to see it was Maggie. Her face was bruised and bloody and her lip was cut. At least she was breathing, but shallowly.

Branyrd went out to the bathroom and picked up a towel from the cabinet under the sink and wet it with cold water. She went back to the room and washed off Maggie's face gently saying a prayer that she would be okay.

A voice came into her head from the LORD. "You must take care of this woman. Watch over her. Someone wants to kill her. He has already injured her as you can see. You will have to watch over her and her daughter to make sure this doesn't happen again."

"Yes, LORD. I will do all I can with your help. Who is this person who wants her dead? Where is he? Can he come here?"

"Yes, to your question. He will come there and try again. When Maggie wakes up, she will tell you who he is and where to find him."

Annie watched Branyrd as she spoke with no one in the room. She waited for Branyrd to stop talking to ask her a question. "Who are you talking to? Will you help my mother?"

"Yes, I will. I am talking to myself, child. I am thinking over what I must do. Do you know who hurt your mother?"

Annie began to cry again and shook her head.

"It's okay. You don't have to tell me until you are ready. I will wait for your mother to wake up to ask her. Why don't you lay down and rest until then? Are you hungry?"

The little girl nodded and sniffled. "Yes. I want waffles for breakfast. They have some downstairs."

"Okay. You stay here and I will go downstairs and get you some. Okay? If your mother wakes up, tell her I will be right back to talk to her."

Annie nodded and sat next to her mother on the bed. She laid down next to her and put her arm across her mother's back.

Branyrd hurried downstairs to the dining room and grabbed a few waffles along with butter and syrup and a carton of milk.

Greta waved at her to come sit with her and the others. The angel walked over and said, "Sorry, I have to get back to my room. I was just going to eat quickly and then go out. I have a lot to do today. Maybe later we can play Monopoly again."

"Okay, see you later, Branyrd." Greta nodded at her and continued eating and talking with the others at the table as before.

Branyrd let out a breath she had been unconsciously holding and hurried back to Annie and her mother.

Annie opened the door once she knew it was Branyrd. She took the plate of waffles from her eagerly and ate at the desk.

Maggie was beginning to wake up. She moaned, sat up and looked at Branyrd in shock. "What are you doing here? Where is my daughter?"

"I am right here, Mommy. The nice lady got me breakfast. I was hungry. Daddy didn't feed me yesterday."

Maggie felt her face and cried out. "I need to get out of here. He will find us. He knows where we are now."

"Who will find you, Maggie?"

"Nate. He is my husband. He picked Annie up from school. I had to go to his house to get her. He is the one who did this to me. I finally hit him over the head with a vase, grabbed Annie and came here. I think he knows where we are now."

"Don't worry, Maggie. I will protect you and Annie."

"How can you do that. You are just a wisp of a girl. He will hurt you too if you get in the way. He wants Annie. He won't stop until he gets her away from me," Maggie cried as she held her face together because of the pain.

Branyrd could see how distressed she was and wanted to take away all her pain. She looked toward the ceiling and whispered. "Please let me take away her pain and fix her face, LORD."

Maggie looked at Branyrd and asked, "Who are you talking to?"

Annie stopped eating and responded, "She did that before, Mommy. She was talking to the ceiling just like that."

"Oh, when I am upset and need help. I always look up at...well, you know about Heaven, don't you?"

"Yes," Maggie responded and continued, "HE doesn't listen to me. I used to pray and go to church. But look what happened to me. Now Nate will take my daughter away from me."

"No, he won't!" Branyrd spoke firmly, louder than she usually did. "As for GOD, HE does listen. That is why I am here to help you."

"What? How can you help me? Look at you! You...you are only a little over five feet tall, if that, Branyrd. You are delicate. He...he will destroy you," Maggie sputtered.

"No, he won't. I promise you, Maggie. I am here to make sure you and Annie are safe. Okay? In fact, I am five feet, six inches tall, to be exact, or least I was in Hea...." Branyrd stopped herself from saying more.

Annie stood next to her mother's bedside and said, "I believe her, Mommie. I like her sparkly sneakers. They are my favorite color too – purple!"

Maggie smiled even though it hurt her face. She patted her daughter on the head. "Yes, dear. If you believe her, then so do I. And, I like Branyrd's sneakers too!"

Branyrd put her arms around both Maggie and Annie and prayed that she would be strong enough to complete this difficult mission ahead.

She waved her hands and said a silent prayer to HIM over Maggie's face to ease the pain she was feeling and stop the bleeding of her lip and eyebrow. Branyrd dabbed around Maggie's face to clean up the rest of the dried blood.

"My face doesn't hurt as much, Branyrd. What did you do?"

"Oh, it wasn't me. HE did that for you. HE does listen. Always remember that. If you pray, HE will listen."

"See, Mommie. Branyrd must be an angel like in church."

"How old are you, Annie?" Branyrd smiled at her and opened her arms.

"I am five." Annie stepped into Branyrd's arms as she whispered into her ear, "I know you are an angel, Branyrd. Where are your wings?"

Branyrd shrugged and smiled at Annie. She whispered, "I left them in Heaven."

CHAPTER TWELVE

In a small bathroom in a rented apartment not far from town, Nate, Maggie's husband, wiped the blood off his hands and held an ice pack to his head. He was a large man, beefy and overweight and strong enough to hurt someone if he wanted to. He had wanted to hurt Maggie. He shouldn't have hit her so hard. He just couldn't control his temper when she told him it was over. He wanted to see his daughter. She was not going to take Annie away from him. He couldn't control himself when he had too much to drink.

Nate had an appointment to meet with his parole officer. He thoroughly checked over his hands before going out the door. He couldn't be late. It would jeopardize his chances to be a father. Maggie had threatened to take Annie away from him forever. But he knew where she was staying. He had followed her there after she had picked up Annie from school one day. He would play it safe for now but he was going to take his daughter and run away as far as he could go. Not even his parole officer would find them.

He thought back to the time he and Maggie had first met at a social dance in town. She was lovely but shy and tried to hide behind a pillar at the back of the dance hall. He had slowly walked over and extended his hand toward her. She looked at him with frightened eyes and shook her head.

He wouldn't take no for an answer and kept his hand extended. After a few minutes of pleading with his eyes she placed her hand in his and moved toward the dance floor.

"Hi. My name is Nate. What's yours?"

The lovely lady dropped her head and whispered, "I'm Maggie."

"Nice to meet you, Maggie. Why are you so shy?" Nate watched her eyes as she looked up at him. He felt like he had been hit by a boulder when their eyes met and he saw their color, a brilliant blue. He felt jitters in the pit of his stomach.

Maggie quickly lowered her head when she felt a little queasy feeling begin. She dropped his hands and rushed to the bathroom. She couldn't meet his eyes. He pleaded with her as she ran away, "What's wrong, Maggie?"

She had not been able to be near a man since her father had…It felt like ages ago. But it still stayed with her. The idea of being close to a man made her sick to her stomach. She was nearly eighteen now, old enough to escape her parent's home, her father's abuse, and run away.

Her mother never believed what her husband had been doing to Maggie since she was only ten years old. Maggie would never be able to convince her mother of her father's abuse to her. She had given up trying. It was time to leave.

Maggie left the bathroom and didn't look around to see if Nate was there waiting for her to return. She told her girlfriends she wasn't feeling well and had to leave. She grabbed her coat and pocketbook and caught a cab home. She only hoped her father would be drunk enough to have fallen asleep.

When she opened the door as quietly as she could, she saw her mother at the kitchen sink washing dishes. She asked, "Is Dad here?"

"Oh, hi Maggie. Did you have a nice time tonight?"

"Umm, yeah. Where's Dad?"

"Oh, he went out with some of his buddies to the local pub to have a few. I don't expect him home for a while. Are you hungry? I still have some leftover lasagna."

"No thank you, Mom." She went to her room to pack her things.

"Are you all right, Maggie?" her mother's voice followed her down the hall.

"Yes, Mom. I'm fine." When her mother didn't say anything else, Maggie peeked out. Her mother was sitting in her lounger with the TV on watching her favorite shows. Now was the time to escape.

Maggie picked up her suitcase with everything she could carry and left the house. She didn't know where she was going. She walked to the bus stop.

***

Nate watched Maggie leave the hall. He followed close behind in his car. He now knew where she lived. He sat back and waited to see if she would come out again. He didn't have to wait long.

Where was she going in such a hurry? He mused. She dragged a large heavy suitcase but walked with a purpose. He stayed back and kept following her. She stopped when she arrived at the bus stop.

Nate casually passed by her and stopped a little ahead and parked his car. He walked back to the bus stop seat and sat next to her.

"Where are you going, Maggie?"

She was shocked to see this man she had just met at the dance here next to her. "I'm going away."

"Where are you going? Can I help you?"

"No, I need to get away?"

"Are you in danger?"

"I…I can't…" Tears flowed as she covered her face with her hands and her shoulders shook.

Nate placed his hand on her shoulder and gave it gentle pressure. "What can I do to help you?"

Maggie shook her head and said, "No one can help me."

"Try me. We all have our problems, Maggie. Do you know that I was arrested for shoplifting? I didn't do any time but had to do public service."

Maggie looked up at Nate with her brilliant blue eyes that glistened with tears.

He had her attention now. She listened to his story. "I was in a store with my friends. They pushed me into stealing a candy bar. They ran away but I got caught red-handed."

"Your friends left you? Did they shoplift too?"

"Yes, they did. They took more than just a candy bar too. I was the unlucky one. But I learned my lesson and will never do that again. I was just sixteen."

"How old are you now, Nate?"

"Don't you know it isn't nice to ask a man's age, Maggie?" he chuckled when he saw her eyes widen.

"Oh, I'm sorry, Nate."

"That's okay, Maggie. I was only kidding. I'm twenty."

"I'm eighteen and old enough to leave home," Maggie countered.

"Hmm, I see. Do you have somewhere to stay when you get wherever you are going?"

"No, I didn't get that far with my plans."

"Won't your parents be worried about you? Did you tell them you are leaving?"

"No...I didn't. I don't want them to find me."

"That is strange. Did they hurt you in any way?"

Maggie looked at Nate and the tears began to fall once again.

He put his arm around her shoulders and told her, "You are coming home with me, Maggie. I will make sure no one hurts you ever again."

**

They had been together since then. When Maggie got pregnant, he married her to give the child a name. Married life wasn't what Nate expected though. HE felt confined to the house with her and the baby. He started to go out with friends to bars and drinking until all hours. That's when the trouble began. That was a little over five years ago.

CHAPTER THIRTEEN

Maggie sat up and sighed. "I'm sorry my daughter bothered you, Branyrd. I wanted you to meet Annie but not like this. Please forgive me."

"It's not a problem, Maggie. I'm here to help you and Annie in any way I can. Do you want to tell me something about your husband?"

"Nate? He...he was once a good man until he started drinking and taking drugs. He rescued me from my father who...Um, this isn't something I can talk about with Annie here."

"I see. That's okay, Maggie. We can talk more about this later. Okay? Why don't you rest some more? I will get you something to eat then take Annie to my room. Okay?"

"Oh, Branyrd. I don't want to impose. But thank you," Maggie said and sighed deeply.

Turning to Annie, Branyrd said, "Why don't you come with me to pick up something for your Mommie to eat and drink?"

"Okay. We'll be right back, Mommy. We will take care of you." Annie smiled and took Branyrd's hand.

Maggie responded with a tear-filled voice, "Thank you, Branyrd. I appreciate this. You are my only friend. Well, I guess we can call ourselves new friends. Right?"

"Yes, most definitely, Maggie. We are friends."

Branyrd turned and went downstairs with Annie holding tightly to her hand. She looked down at the little girl and asked, "Are you okay, Annie?"

"I'm okay. I don't like my Daddy. He hit my mommy real hard. She fell down when he did that. I was afraid to get near him. He might hit me too. Then Mommy hit him with the glass thing."

"No one is going to hurt you or your mommy ever again. You are safe in my care."

"Thank you, Branyrd. You are an angel, aren't you?" Annie smiled up into the angel's face.

"Well, let me tell you a secret, Annie. Maybe I am. But no one else should know. Can you keep a secret just between the two of us?"

"Oh, yes. I am the best secret keeper. I never share a secret with anyone else. I promise. Pinkie-swear?"

"Okay, pinkie-swear." Branyrd gripped Annie's extended pinkie and shook it.

Annie winked at the angel and giggled.

"What's so funny, Annie?"

"I never pinkie-sweared with an angel before."

"I never pinkie-sweared with a little girl before. But remember, Annie, this is a secret between you and me."

"Yes, but I did tell my mommy that I thought you were an angel. Is that okay?"

"Hmm. Did she believe you?" Branyrd asked with a furrowed brow.

"No, she just laughed at me and said that you were a very nice person."

"Oh, I see." Branyrd relaxed and smiled at Annie.

They both laughed until they arrived in the dining area and got in line for some food.

"Can I have some fruit, Branyrd? I ate all my waffles but am still a little hungry."

"Of course, Annie. You can have whatever you want. Here, take a plate and put your choices in it."

"Thank you, Branyrd." Annie squeezed the angel's hand before picking up a plate and proceeding to fill it to the brim.

They went back upstairs and sat while Maggie and Annie ate. Maggie looked a little better now and her face was less swollen and red. Her eyes were brighter and clearer as she looked at Branyrd with a smile.

"I can't thank you enough, Branyrd, for doing this. I didn't know what I was going to do. I didn't put in for other meals besides breakfast. I have been trying to save some money so I can take Annie away from here."

"Well, I am here if you need anything at all. I will make sure that both of you are well fed. Don't worry about that."

Maggie sniffed away some new tears as she went toward Branyrd and put out her arms. Branyrd stepped into her embrace and hugged Maggie back. The angel sent her thoughts to HIM to give this poor woman some comfort and lessen her pain.

HE whispered back to Branyrd in her head, "It is already done, Angel First Class. Good job."

Branyrd whispered back, "Thank you, LORD!"

The angel was beaming as their embrace ended and she patted Annie on the head. Annie had joined the hugging and was still holding onto her mother's leg.

"I will go back to my room. If you need me any more today, please knock on my door and I will come right away," Branyrd stated as she turned to go.

"Please don't leave yet, Branyrd. Why don't you get yourself something to eat and join us here? I'd like to talk to you some more."

"Okay, Maggie. I am all set. I already had something to eat earlier. Not hungry now. But I will get a cup of coffee. I really like coffee. I never had any in…before."

"Really? You never had coffee before, Branyrd? Do you prefer tea or soda or something else?"

"Um, no. I like to try different things. But I think I like coffee the best." Branyrd excused herself and went downstairs to get her coffee. She shook her head and sighed. "I almost gave myself away by saying Heaven, LORD, again."

When Branyrd got back to Maggie's room she sat down on the other twin bed with Annie's permission and sipped her newfound love, coffee.

After Maggie had finished eating she began by saying to Branyrd, "I'd like to tell you a little bit about Nate. Like I said before he was once a good, kind man. After I had Annie, he became restless and went out every night with his friends. I guess being tied down was too much for him with the responsibility of taking care of us too. I left home at eighteen because my family home was no longer a good fit for me. I tried to discuss this with my mother but she never wanted to listen. She was content with my father and didn't believe whatever I said about him and his mistreatment of me."

"I see. You don't have to go any farther than that. I can surmise what you mean. I think. Did you parents try to find you?"

"No, we moved away from them. I guess they didn't miss me enough to try to find me. I cut ties and never looked back. I don't even know if they are still alive," Maggie sighed.

"Sorry to hear that, Maggie. But what were you going to do on your own if you hadn't had help from Nate?"

"I really hadn't given it much thought. I was going to find a place to stay and get a job. Each day would have been a new day for me. I would have survived, I think. But I hadn't planned on having a family so soon. Annie is my little angel, though. She is sweet, kind and nothing like her.... Well, you know what I mean. I love her so much. All I want to do is take care of her and make sure she has a better life than I had."

"Well, I know you will succeed in doing just that, Maggie. Don't worry too much. I will help you along the way. We are, after all, friends. That's what friends do, help each other."

"Thank you, Branyrd. You really are a special person. Where did you come from? I wish I had met you a long time ago. I could have used your kind heart back then. Are you married? Children?"

"Thank you, Maggie. No, I do not have a husband or children. But I do have a lot of friends in high places."

"High places? Are you influential?"

"Influential? Oh, do you mean of money?" Branyrd giggled after she received a silent message from Benedicto with an explanation of what influential meant.

"Oh no. I do not have any money. But I have something worth more than money. I have faith."

"Faith? Are you a church goer, you mean? You believe in God?"

"Yes, to my beliefs. I don't go to church as such but to a higher power I celebrate my faith."

"A higher power?"

"Oh, I mean I pray to the LORD. HE answers all prayers, Maggie. You must put your faith in HIM to get you through the toughest times. I do."

"Have you had some tough times too, Branyrd?"

Branyrd laughed, "Well, my tough times are nothing like yours, Maggie. I just got into trouble when I was younger and in a different class. Now I have grown up and am more reliable."

"A different class? I don't understand."

"Oh, never mind. It isn't important. What is important is that you get better and heal. Say a prayer to HIM tonight before you go to sleep. In the morning all will be much better. I assure you. Now, I think you should get some rest."

"Yes, I think you are right, Branyrd. Thank you again. "

"Why don't you rest now. I will make sure that Annie gets lunch and dinner."

"Oh, Branyrd, you don't need to do that."

"Yes, I do, Maggie. I promised to make sure you both were fed more than just breakfast.

"Thank you again, Branyrd." Maggie laid down on her twin bed and closed her eyes.

Before Branyrd could leave Maggie's' room, Annnie rushed up to the angel and held onto her, preventing her from leaving.

"What's wrong, little one?"

"I don't want you to leave. Can I go back to your room while my mommy sleeps? I am not sleepy yet. It is too early for my bedtime."

"Of course, I planned to take care of you and make sure you have lunch and dinner while your mother rests."

"Really? You will take care of me, Branyrd?"

Maggie looked up from her bed and nodded. "It's okay for you to go with Branyrd, but you must come back by seven, Annie. I don't want you to take any more time from Branyrd. She has been too kind and attentive already. You must give her some space."

"Okay, Mommy. Thank you. I promise to come back at seven. What can we do now, Branyrd?" Annie anxiously put her hand into the angel's.

"It's no problem, Maggie. Come with me, Annie. We can play cards or I can teach you how to play Monopoly."

"Are we going to your room, Branyrd?"

"No, we will go downstairs to the living area with the card tables. They have games, cards and fun stuff to do there. Do you want anything else to eat or drink, Annie?"

"Yes. Can I have some ice cream?"

"I don't see why not as long as it doesn't take away your appetite for lunch. Let's go get some first. What flavor do you like?"

"Don't worry. I always have room for lunch, Branyrd. Oh, I love chocolate with sprinkles!"

"Okay chocolate with sprinkles, it is. Maybe I will try some too." Branyrd smiled. She felt like a kid again being with this delightful little girl.

CHAPTER FOURTEEN

The LORD watched over Branyrd, Angel First Class, as she went about her mission with Maggie and her daughter, Annie. HE smiled as HE discussed the case with Benedicto, Angel First Class on High.

On High meant Benedicto was higher than the other angels First Class. Only four other angels were higher. They were Michael, Gabriel, Raphael and Uriel. They were Archangels.

"She is doing quite well, LORD. Don't you think so?" Benedicto asked with a little hesitancy.

"Yes, she is doing a wonderful job so far. I have faith in her to do this job. I knew she was capable enough. She is learning a lot on her own also. She hasn't asked you for too many explanations, Benedicto, has she?"

"No. She hasn't so far. I, too, am pleased with her performance, LORD."

"She has a kind heart, so to speak, if not a soul," the LORD laughed out loud as HE said this. "Of course, she doesn't have a heart or soul. But if she did, they would both be perfect."

"Oh, yes, LORD," Benedicto smiled but did not laugh for fear he would laugh too hard and long and offend HIM. He knew HE had a good sense of humor but could become annoyed if one laughed too long or hard at one of HIS jokes. At least he thought HE would be offended. He never wanted to cross HIM and find out, though, as kind and benevolent as the LORD was.

"Keep a close eye on Branyrd, Benedicto. There will be some rough times ahead for her in this mission. I know she will do all she can to succeed but she doesn't know yet about the White Stag Gang. They could cause her trouble."

"Yes, LORD. I will be on alert at all times and close by if needed." Benedicto bowed to HIM and left to return to watch over this new Angel First Class in his charge.

***

Annie and Branyrd sat at the long table with a few other any women while they ate their ice cream cones after they had dinner.

Branyrd looked at Annie with a kind smile and asked, "Are you enjoying your ice cream?"

"Oh, yes, Branyrd! It's my favorite and I can't get enough. My daddy used to take me out for an ice cream but now that he …" Annie sniffled and stopped licking her ice cream.

"Annie, it's okay, sweetheart. I understand. Your daddy is sorry about doing that, I'm sure. But for the meantime you need to be close to your mommy and help take care of her. Okay? I will be here also to help you both."

"Will you? Can I come over to your room and see you anytime I want?" Annie looked at the angel with wide and eager eyes.

"Of course. You are welcome to come visit me anytime as long as you ask your mommy for permission first. We don't want her to worry about you. She needs to get better. Okay?"

"Yes, I understand, Branyrd. I will take good care of her. Can I ask you a question, Branyrd?"

"What is it, little one?"

"Well, who is going to take me back and forth to school while Mommy is sick?"

"Oh, yes. I almost forgot about that. I will take you, Annie. I can walk you there and back each day. It's not too far from here. That's why your mommy took a room here to be close to your school."

Annie smiled and continued licking her ice cream which was now running down the side of her cone. "I would really like that, Branyrd. You can meet some of my friends or at least some who I want to have as friends."

Branyrd listened to what Annie said about friends. "Don't you have any friends?" The angel was worried about this fact.

"I…umm. Not really. I want them to be my friends but they make fun of me because I don't have a house and live at the YWCA."

"Really? Did they say that to you, Annie?"

"Well, kinda. I can't invite them to come to my house because I don't have a house. They know where I live. They have seen me walking here. I want to invite them for my birthday, but I don't think they will want to come here."

"Well, why don't you want to invite them here? You have a big play area with lots of games and a place to get all kinds of food and ice cream. I bet they don't have that."

Annie giggled. "I guess they don't."

"When is your birthday, Annie?"

"It's next Wednesday. But I don't need to have a party or any gifts. It's okay. No one would want to come here. Besides, my mother can't do anything. She is too hurt and sick right now."

"That is true but you do have a new friend who can do all of that for you."

"I do?"

"Yes, you do."

"Who is that?" Annie asked as she lifted her brows and looked at Branyrd.

"Well, what about me? Aren't I your new friend?"

"Ha, ha! Yes, I guess you are. Would you do that for me? Help me have a birthday party?"

"Of course, I will. That is what friends are for, Annie."

"Oh, thank you so much, Branyrd. You are the best new friend anyone could ever have!" Annie put down her ice cream cone and hugged the angel tightly as if she didn't want to ever let go.

Branyrd felt tears brimming as she hugged Annie back and sighed. "I will be honored to give you the best birthday party you ever had." The angel had no idea what she would have to do though. She shook her head and thought, *I have some higher help that will know what to do.*

"Thank you!" Annie jumped up and down, forgetting about her melting ice cream which Branyrd tossed into the nearest trash container.

"But first we need to talk to your mother and get her permission. I'm sure she won't mind me helping put this together."

Annie looked anxious all of a sudden hearing this and responded meekly, "What if Mom doesn't want to let you help?"

"Don't worry, little one. Let's talk to her now. Okay? It is almost time for you to go back anyway."

"Okay, Branyrd. Let's go." Annie raced back upstairs to her room and knocked on the door.

The door was opened quickly by her mother who was looking a lot less swollen and black and blue in the face. Maggie smiled as she saw her daughter and Branyrd. She knew something was up because Annie was having a difficult time keeping herself from bouncing up and down.

"Hi Mommy! I had some more ice cream with sprinkles with Branyrd. It was so good! Can we talk to you, Mommy? Are you feeling better?"

"Yes, to both questions, Annie. Come sit down on the edge of my bed and talk to me."

Branyrd sat in the desk chair and waited for Annie to ask her questions.

Annie exchanged a worried glance with Branyrd, and after seeing her nod, she asked her first question.

"Mommy, can I have a birthday party next week? My birthday is on Wednesday, you know."

"Umm...well, we'll see."

Annie looked at Branyrd and sighed. "Branyrd, can you ask my mommy now?"

Branyrd came close to the bed and sat down on the other twin bed and cleared her throat.

"Maggie, I would like to help you with Annie's party. If you don't mind. I can do all the leg work, shopping and arranging for invitations."

"Really? You would do all that, Branyrd? You hardly know us! I can't expect you to take on all that. I was planning to take Annie to the park and out to have an ice cream. That is all I can manage at this time."

Annie dropped her head in disappointment as she went out of the room and closed the door so no one would see her tears. A door down the hall was heard closing with a bang, most likely the bathroom.

CHAPTER FIFTEEN

"I'm sorry, Maggie. I didn't want to upset either of you. I really would like to do this for you and Annie. I know what a difficult time you are both having with your husband and all."

"I appreciate what you want to do. But I cannot let you do all this. Annie would expect it and more from you. What will happen after you leave here? It would be harder on her then."

"I don't plan on leaving any time soon, Maggie. I am here to help you as long as you need me." Branyrd whispered in her head, *or as long as HE allows me to stay.*

"How did you know it was Annie's birthday next week?"

"I asked her."

"Oh, I see."

"Please let me do this for her and you. It will be fun. I have a friend who knows about these things and will help me. You won't have to do anything but concentrate on healing and getting back to your healthy self."

"Well, I guess if you insist. But you must let me do something. I could write out invitations with Annie."

"Okay. That sounds good. Where do I get these invitations?" Branyrd was feeling way out of her comfort zone but wanted to do this for Annie.

"Annie and I will make some. I am feeling much better, Branyrd. You mustn't do too much. I don't want Annie to expect this every year. I don't know what will happen next year. I may not have much more money than I do now."

"Let's not worry about the future for now, Maggie. We will take one day at a time. Okay?"

"Okay. But I need to begin work at the diner tomorrow. I just heard from the owner. I had applied for the position of waitress but wasn't sure that I would get it. Now I can pay for our room and not have to sweep floors here. But I can't go looking like this. Will you help me cover up all this with my makeup?"

Branyrd looked at Maggie and said, "I don't know how to do that. I have never used makeup before."

"That's okay. I will tell you what to do, Branyrd. You can use some too, if you want, not that you need it. You are beautiful, Branyrd."

"Thank you, Maggie. But no. I can't use makeup. I mean. That is not for me. But I will help you if you tell me how to do that, Maggie."

Branyrd learned how to apply makeup that day. She felt quite proud of her work after looking at Maggie. There was no sign of any bruising on her face. In fact, Maggie looked quite beautiful.

"You look lovely, Maggie. I didn't realize how beautiful you are," Branyrd gushed.

"Thank you, Branyrd. I think you did a wonderful job for a first-time makeup artist. I better go see about Annie. She needs to apologize for her abrupt absence and behavior. That is unacceptable."

"Let me go get her, Maggie."

Branyrd knocked on the bathroom door and waited for Annie to answer. "Are you in there, Annie? It's Branyrd. Come back to your room. Your mother has something to tell you."

Annie stuck her head out and wiped away the tears that were still flowing. "What does she want to tell me, Branyrd? That I can't have a party?"

"I can't tell you. Your mother wants to share something with you. Come along now. Wipe those tears." Branyrd put out her hand and Annie slipped her smaller one there.

"Okay," Annie sniffled and sighed as she moved along with Branyrd.

Maggie was standing at the door of her room and welcomed them in. "Sit down, Annie. I have something to say to you."

"Yes, Mommy," Annie said, sighed heavily and wiped her wet face with her sleeve.

"Listen to me, Annie. First of all, I expect an apology for your rude behavior just now. Apologize to Branyrd."

"I'm sorry, Branyrd, for leaving like that and slamming the door closed. I was angry."

"That's okay, Annie. I understand you were disappointed about your party."

"Now Annie, I have something else to say to you. Branyrd and I will organize your birthday party for next Wednesday."

Before Maggie could say another word Annie jumped up and down and screamed with joy. "Thank you, Mommy and Branyrd! Thank you so much!" She squeezed her mother tightly and went toward the Angel. Branyrd was nearly knocked over by Annie's running hug.

Branyrd said with a laugh, "You are welcome, Annie. But we need your help also. You need to give us a list of how many friends you want to have. That way we will know how many are coming to your party."

"I can do that. But what about invitations? I need to give them invitations."

"Of course, sweetie," Maggie responded. "You and I will make some, okay?"

"How are we going to make some, Mommy?"

"Well, we will need some colored paper, scissors, pens or markers. We can draw a cake or balloons on each one or whatever you want to draw."

"Yes, I like that! I can draw really good, Mommy!"

"Yes, you can, Annie." Her mother felt her heart lighten just to see her daughter so happy. She had missed this.

Branyrd looked at the joy in Annie's face and almost cried. "I can go find some of those things for you. Okay?"

The Angel excused herself and went back to her room to seek Benedicto's help.

"Benedicto, are you there? I need your help."

In the blink of an eye Benedicto appeared in front of Branyrd. "What do you need, Branyrd?"

She explained to him about her promise to help organize a birthday party. She had no idea what to do first. Benedicto smiled and patted her on the head. "Don't worry, little angel. I will help you."

"The first thing you will need is the invitations. You can either purchase them or make them yourself."

"Yes, that is what Annie and Maggie are going to do. I have to get some colored paper, scissors and pens or markers for them. Can you find them for me?"

"Here they are for you. I don't need to go to the store. What else do you require?"

Out of thin air the materials appeared. Branyrd smiled and shook her head in surprise. "I should have known you would do that, Benedicto!" Branyrd guffawed.

"I don't know what I will need. This is the first birthday party I have ever organized, Benedicto. You know that. Stop it!" Branyrd was thinking something more unbecoming of an angel to say and had to wash out her thoughts quickly before HE scolded her.

Benedicto couldn't help but laugh heartily at Branyrd's stricken face. "I know, little angel. I was only teasing you. Sorry about that."

"Okay. Here is what you will need to do. Benedicto made a list and put it on the desk for Branyrd to look at."

"I need balloons? What are balloons? Cake and ice cream I know about already. They are delicious!"

"Balloons are large rubber objects filled with air. You blow them up or you can purchase them all blown up already in a store."

"How do you know all this stuff, Benedicto? Have you ever had a birthday party?"

"No, of course not, Branyrd. But the LORD tells me everything I need to know about things on Earth. One day you will know everything too. But all in good time, little angel."

"Okay, I guess I have to wait until then. But you will help me through all this, won't you, Benedicto?"

"Of course. That is why I am here, Branyrd. I am here to help you with your mission. How is it coming?"

"Oh, good. I think it's coming along. But, wait a minute, Benedicto. You already know all about that. Don't you?"

Benedicto didn't answer for he was no longer in the room.

CHAPTER SIXTEEN

"Now where did he go? I can't believe this. What do I do now? I don't know where there is a store. I wouldn't know what to do when I got there either," Branyrd sighed.

"I will go with you, Branyrd."

The little angel jumped back in alarm when she heard Benedicto's voice but didn't see him behind her.

"Why do you do that, Benedicto? You are always sneaking up on me! If angels could die from fright, I would have been a goner a long time ago!"

"You are a funny one, little angel," Benedicto tittered as he covered his mouth to keep the laugh from getting too loud.

"I am serious, First Class Angel on High! We need to go to the store and get all the supplies for the party. It is only three days away. Please help me. I am so nervous and want it all to go well for Annie. She is so excited about it."

"I understand, Branyrd. Okay. Let's go shopping."

With a wave of his hand, he whisked them both out of the building and in front of a store that was nearby the YWCA.

"Oh, I didn't expect to go this way. I thought we were going to act like humans and walk there."

"Well, you did sound like you were in a hurry, little angel. So here we are. Look at your list and we will find the items you need. I could have whipped them up in the room for you. But you didn't look too happy when I did that with the paper, pens and markers."

"I wasn't expecting that. That would have been a lot easier than shopping. But now that we are here, let's do it." Branyrd walked into the store with her list in hand and looked around.

She stopped in the first aisle and turned around to look for Benedicto. Of course, he wasn't there.

"Now where did he go again?" Branyrd sighed in exasperation.

"This way, little Angel. Our first item is right here."

Branyrd bristled at Benedicto as he reappeared in front of her and took the first item off the shelf. It was a package of different sizes of balloons in pretty colors of pink, purple, green and blue.

"Annie will love these! What else do I need?" She looked down at her list again.

"Candles and a cake and ice cream. Can I get these here too?" She looked around and didn't see any.

"Don't worry, Branyrd. I will get them for you. There is a bakery on another aisle and ice cream at yet another one. Here we are. Look, see all the cakes in the glassed case?"

"Ooh, yes. They look delicious!" Branyrd looked over each one and chose the one with the pinkest frosting on it. Next, she picked up some pink candles to match the cake.

The little angel strolled along pushing her carriage that suddenly had appeared in front of her to place the cake. She found some freezer sections with ice cream. Her head was spinning with all the choices. But she chose two kinds – chocolate and vanilla after Benedicto said they were the most popular.

Once they reached the cash register, Benedicto took over and handled the transactions. In a snap of his fingers, they were back at the Y in Branyrd's room.

"Now we must get this cake and ice cream into a freezer to keep them fresh, Branyrd."

"Why is that, Benedicto?"

"Well, the ice cream will melt into a puddle if we don't. Let me get you a small refrigerator/freezer so you can keep them for Annie until her party."

A small white object appeared in the corner of Branyrd's room next to her desk. She opened the door and looked inside. The cake and ice cream were already there.

"That was fast, Benedicto. I didn't even see you do that."

"That is my job, Branyrd, to do things quickly and efficiently. Time is wasting here on Earth. In Heaven we don't worry about time. There is no such thing as time."

"I know. I have to get used to this time factor, months, days, hours, minutes and seconds. There's too much to think about all the time. I don't know how these humans do this."

Branyrd looked around and once again she was talking to herself. She picked up the colored paper, pens and markers and brought them over to Maggie and Annie so they could begin creating the invitations.

Maggie smiled when she saw Branyrd with her arms full of the supplies. "Thank you so much, Branyrd. You are such a kind and thoughtful person. How lucky can we get?"

Branyrd laughed and said, "I don't know if luck had anything to do with me being here. Umm… I mean. Thank you for saying that. I feel fortunate to have met you both too. It's almost as if we have known each other for a long time."

"Yes, I agree, Branyrd. I still think we are lucky. I feel as if you brought this luck with you from wherever you came. I thank you for helping us and just being here. I don't know what we would have done without your help at this time. So many bad things have come to pass lately but now I feel as if the sun is shining upon us."

"I think so too. It has been much brighter lately. I guess HE must be pleased with me."

"What did you say, Branyrd?" Maggie looked up from the invitations she and Annie were now creating.

"Oh, nothing, Maggie. All is well. If you finish all the invitations, Annie can give them out to all her friends at school tomorrow."

"Yes, I can't wait to do that, Branyrd. Thank you so much for getting the supplies for us."

"Mommy, what about a cake and ice cream? Are you going to buy some for my party?"

Maggie looked crestfallen at this and glanced at Branyrd who winked at her and nodded. "All set, Annie. I already picked some up. It's in my refrigerator/freezer in my room."

"You have a freezer in your room, Branyrd?" Maggie asked in surprise.

"Well, my friend bought one for me to put the cake and ice cream in."

Annie asked, ignoring the conversation about a refrigerator, "Oh, can I see the cake?"

"Annie, you can look at it on your birthday. That way it will be a surprise to you and your friends at the same time."

"Okay, Mommy. Will it have my name and 'happy birthday' on it?"

Branyrd's eyes opened wide. She hadn't done that. She would have to somehow put Annie's name and 'happy birthday' on the cake. How was she going to do that?

The angel excused herself and said she needed to go to her room to rest. They were so busy they hadn't noticed that Branyrd had left their room.

Back in her own room she opened the refrigerator and gasped in shock. On top of the cake, it read 'Happy Birthday Annie.'

She smiled and looked around but Benedicto was nowhere in sight. He had heard them and had taken care of the cake for her.

Branyrd sighed in relief. What would she do without her First Class Angel on High?

CHAPTER SEVENTEEN

Annie went to school excited to see all the kids, share her news about her party and pass out the invitations.

She waited for recess before she did this. The first person she went up to was Grace. Grace was the most popular girl in her class. Everyone wanted her as a friend including Annie. When Annie got closer to Grace, the girl turned her back on her and walked away. She didn't even give Annie a chance to share her news or give her an invitation.

Annie sighed and turned to another classmate. This one was Robert. He was busy talking to his other friends and didn't glance up when Annie called out to him. He and his friends walked away ignoring her.

Annie kept trying to give others her invitations but they didn't give her a chance to share them. She could feel tears prickling and tried to hold them back.

Another little girl, Deidra, came over to her. Deidra was a quiet person and a little shy like Annie.

Deidra cleared her throat and asked, "Are you all right, Annie? What do you have in your hand?"

Annie sniffled and wiped the tears that were coming down her face. "Oh, my birthday is on Wednesday and I just wanted to invite some friends to my party. But no one wants to talk to me."

"Don't worry. I will come to your party. If you invite me, that is," Deidra smiled and put her hand out to accept the invitation.

Annie's face lit up and she placed an invitation in Deidra's hand. "Do you really want to come to my party, Deidra?"

"Oh yes. I love parties but no one ever invites me to theirs. I would love to go to yours, Annie. I will bring you a special present too." Deidra smiled and thought, I have always wanted to have a friend like Annie.

"Thank you, Deidra. Does that mean we are going to be friends?"

"Most definitely, Annie. See you on Wednesday. We need to get back to class now. I can't wait to go to your party."

"Thank you, Deidra. My address is on the invitation. I will meet you at the door and show you the way to my room. I can't wait for it either!"

***

When Annie's mother picked her up at school that afternoon, Annie couldn't wait to tell her mother about her new friend, Deidra.

"Did you pass out your invitations, Annie?" Maggie asked hesitantly as she watched her daughter's face.

"Well, I tried to with several of my classmates but they didn't even look at me. One girl, her name is Deidra, came up to me and asked for an invitation. She said she saw the others not taking them."

"Oh, so sorry about that, Annie. Did you give one to Deidra?"

"Yes, I did, Mommy. She is coming to my party. I don't care if she is the only one."

"That's good, Annie At least you have a new friend, Deidra. She sounds like a nice little girl."

"I think Deidra and I will become best friends. I like her."

When they arrived back at their room in the YWCA Annie asked, "Mommy, can I go tell Branyrd about Deidra?

"Sure. If she is not busy. Come right back after, okay?"

"Okay."

Annie was all smiles when she knocked on Branyrd's door to tell her all about Deidra.

"Hi Annie. Is everything all right?"

"Oh, yes, Branyrd. Guess what?"

"What?" Branyrd matched the smile that was plastered to Annie's little face.

"I have a new friend named, Deidra. She is coming to my birthday party!"

"Wow, that's wonderful, Annie. Who else is coming?"

"Umm…no one else. She is the only one who took an invitation. The rest of the kids didn't even look at me or my invitations. They weren't interested."

Branyrd didn't know what to say.

Annie dropped her head but then quickly perked up again saying, "I don't care if they don't come. I am happy to have Deidra. She and I will be best friends, you know."

"Really? That's great, Annie. I am so happy for you. You will have a wonderful party. Your mom and I will be there too."

"Yes, that means there will be four of us at my party. Can we play games and do fun stuff, Branyrd?"

"Of course. I can teach you how to play Monopoly and a card game that some people here taught me."

"You will? Okay. When can we start? My party is only two days away. I have to learn quickly."

"If your mother says it's okay, we can go downstairs and learn now. I'll pick up some snacks for us too. You must be getting hungry."

"I am always hungry, Branyrd. Thank you." Annie's face lit up at the thought of some snacks.

"Let's go ask your mother if she doesn't mind us doing this now and if she wants anything too." Before Branyrd could say another word, Annie had run out of the room and was back in her own room.

Branyrd sighed, why does everyone disappear on me?

Annie was explaining everything to her mother when Branyrd came to the room. Annie nodded to the angel and raced out of the door once again.

Branyrd smiled and shrugged her shoulders at Maggie but asked before she turned to leave, "Are you okay? Do you need anything, Maggie? I can bring something back for you."

"No thank you, I'm fine., Branyrd. I had a pretty good day at work today. My boss is kind and considerate. She knows about Nate. I think she saw my bruises even with the makeup. She is trying to convince me to go to a shelter for battered women. I feel safe here and don't think that's necessary."

"That might not be a bad idea though, Maggie. Do they offer protection in some way?"

"I guess. They never let the husbands in. They have a bodyguard at the door most days and nights to enforce that."

"That sounds good," Branyrd said but not with much conviction. She was thinking about where she would stand if Maggie did that. This was her mission. Then her mission would be over.

"What's the matter, Branyrd? You look upset. Did I say something wrong? I don't want to go and leave you. You are my only friend."

"Oh, that's not it, Maggie. I would follow you wherever you go. I want to help you and Annie get back on your feet. I have a mission and will not leave until it is completed."

"A mission? What do you mean, Branyrd?"

"Oh, that is just my way of saying I will not abandon you or Annie in your time of need."

"You are too kind, Branyrd. What did we do to deserve a friend like you? You must have friends if not family. Please don't feel as if you have to watch over us. We will be fine. We have been all this time, well almost." Maggie shrugged her shoulders and smiled wanly.

"No problem on my end. I don't have a family as such, as I mentioned before, and my friends are busy with things to do. No one will miss me."

"We are fortunate to have you as long as you plan to stay around, Branyrd. Thank you for taking Annie for a little while. I plan to take a nap. If you get back and I am sleeping, please wake me and we can go down to dinner together. Now that I've got a full-time job, I can afford three meals a day for Annie and me."

"I certainly will, Maggie. Did Annie tell you that I am going to teach her how to play Monopoly and cards?"

"Yes, she is so excited about that and her party. I can't thank you enough for helping organize it, Branyrd. It's too bad she couldn't get more children interested in coming. Kids can be so cruel sometimes. They tend to look down on those who do not have a home of their own. I plan one day to rectify that for Annie. But, in the meantime, we will make do here until I can save up enough to afford a place of our own."

"Well, if you need me to help, I will do what I can, too."

"Oh, Branyrd! You are so kind. Don't worry about us. Please check out what Annie is doing. She might be taking over the whole place by now. Sorry to keep you."

CHAPTER EIGHTEEN

Annie was sitting at a table with three older women who were fawning all over her. They had picked up snacks and juice for her and she was helping herself to everything.

Branyrd smiled and walked over to the table. "What are you doing, Annie? I hope you aren't bothering these ladies."

"Oh, they don't mind. They said they like children."

One woman spoke up, "She is just darling. Is she your daughter?"

"Oh, no. I am just watching over her for her mother for a little while."

"Well, you do look too young to have a child," another woman stated as she looked Branyrd over closely.

"I guess," Branyrd said with a raised eyebrow.

"Branyrd, look I just learned how to play crazy eights. These ladies taught me. It's so much fun! I will have to teach Deidra when she comes for my birthday."

One woman said in surprise, "Your birthday, Annie? When is your birthday, sweet child?"

Annie couldn't wait to tell the ladies all about her birthday and her new friend, Deidra. The ladies indulged her and nodded at the right times and smiled at Branyrd.

Branyrd waited for Annie's diatribe to end before speaking up, "Well, I think you have taken enough of these ladies' time, Annie. Why don't we go over to another table and let the ladies play their games. I can teach you how to play Monopoly at the empty table over there."

Annie excused herself and followed Branyrd to the empty table. She was soon learning how to set up the Monopoly game and winning the game in the process.

"That was so much fun, Branyrd. Thank you. Can we get something to eat now?"

"Yes, let's go wake up your mother and see if she is ready to have dinner with us."

"Okay," Annie said as she sashayed to the table where the three ladies were still playing cards. She leaned over and whispered something in each of their ears. With a smile of satisfaction, she followed Branyrd back to her room.

"What were you saying to the ladies, Annie?"

"Oh, I just told them thank you for teaching me how to play cards and for the nice snacks."

"That was nice of you. You are a thoughtful little girl."

After dinner Branyrd took Annie back to her room so her mother could rest up for work the next day. The angel showed Annie the package of colorful balloons.

"Wow, these are great, Branyrd. Can you help me blow them up on Wednesday before my party?"

"Of course. I never did this before but we can do it together for the first time."

"I don't think I can do it as well as you, though. I am still small and don't have enough breath to blow into it."

"I see what you mean. Maybe because I am bigger, I will have more breath to blow into them. We will see on Wednesday. If we need help, I know someone who can do this for us easily."

"Okay, Branyrd. I can't wait for my party. It's only two days away now!"

"It's time for you to go back to your room and get some sleep. You want to be rested for school, Annie."

Branyrd led the way back to Maggie's room. With Maggie's permission Branyrd tucked Annie in bed after she changed into her pjs and brushed her teeth.

"Goodnight, little one," Branyrd said and waved to Maggie. "See you both tomorrow."

***

Not far away in his cluttered and filthy room Nate lay awake thinking of ways to kidnap Annie. He knew it wouldn't be easy to get into the YWCA without a good reason. He would have to get her at school.

He closed his eyes with a smile as his plan came to him. He would be successful and make Maggie sorry she ever said she wanted to end their marriage.

When morning came, he felt more alive than ever before. He grabbed a cup of coffee after washing out one of the many cups that littered his kitchen. He never washed anything out but today was going to be a good day. He wanted to start out with a fresh cup of coffee to keep him going. He had a lot to do.

His first stop was to pick up a bag of Annie's favorite chocolates. He had to have something with him when he picked her up from school. He had to arrive early and go to the office to tell them that he was picking up Annie instead of her mother. He had a story all set to tell them. He would appear distraught because his wife was in a car accident and couldn't pick their daughter up. He was to bring Annie to the hospital to see her mother right away.

Nate put liquid tears into his eyes before he got to the principal's office to pick up his daughter. He sniffled a few times and let the tears run down his face.

The secretary at the front desk looked up when she heard his sniffling and got up quickly to his side. "Are you all right, sir?"

Nate dabbed at the tears and sniffled for special effect as he shook his head. "No, I need to pick up my daughter, Annie

Preston. My wife…umm…has been in a terrible car accident. I need to take Annie to see her in the hospital."

"Oh, I'm so sorry, Mr. Preston. But you are not on the list to pick Annie up. You were taken off since the last time you picked your daughter up."

Nate leaned over as if he was going to pass out. He shook his head and fake cried. "You can't be serious! I must take her to her mother. My wife could die. She wants to see Annie. I promised her I would do this."

The secretary called the principal on the intercom to come out to deal with this problem.

"Can I help you, sir? I am Principal Harris. What is the problem?"

Nate did the best he could minus the fake tears to show how upset he was about not being able to pick up his daughter. "You must let me pick up Annie. My wife is dying in the hospital and wants to see her. You can't take away my wife's last possible chance to see her daughter, can you?"

The principal and secretary shared a concerned look. The principal whispered to her secretary and told her to call Annie down to the office.

CHAPTER NINETEEN

Benedicto appeared to Branyrd early the next morning. He wore a worried expression on his face.

"Good morning, Benedicto, Angel First Class on High. What are you doing here so early? Would you believe I think I fell asleep like a human? If I stay here much longer, I may become one. Will I?"

Benedicto waited until there was a lull in Branyrd's diatribe before speaking. "Branyrd, you must be prepared for some troubling times ahead. You will be expected to move your mission forward."

"What do you mean, Benedicto? Move my mission forward?"

"There has been a new development. You will hear about it soon. You must act fast and help Maggie and Annie. They are in trouble."

"Trouble? What kind of trouble? What are you talking about, Benedicto? You are getting me exasperated!" Branyrd tried to keep calm and erase all the vulgar language that was now flooding her mind. "Answer me, Benedicto! $#!$!"

"I don't think you meant that, Branyrd," Benedicto said softly as he gazed at her with steel in his eyes.

Annie shook her head and whispered to the LORD, "So sorry, LORD. I didn't mean that. Please forgive me. I am exasperated by Benedicto. He won't tell me what he is talking about?"

"You must listen to him, Branyrd. Never question his words. Pay attention. Something is coming to pass. You must be calm in order to handle it. I will be here to guide you as well as Benedicto."

"Yes, LORD. I will pay attention and listen. But what is it?"

***

Later that afternoon Maggie headed over to pick up Annie from school. Her boss at the diner told her that as long as she worked over the weekends, she could leave at 3:00 each day to pick up her daughter. Maggie would have to impose upon Branyrd once again to help her with Annie on the weekends.

Maggie waited outside as she usually did each day for Annie to come out after the bell. She waited and waited some more but couldn't wait anymore. All the kids were out and still no sign of Annie. She went to the office to see what was keeping her.

"Oh, Mrs. Preston! I thought you were in the hospital. Are you all right?"

"Yes, I am perfectly fine. I am here to pick up my daughter, Annie. Why would you think I was in the hospital?"

The secretary's face turned white and she picked up her phone to call the principal right away.

"Just one moment, Mrs. Preston. I will get Principal Harris to speak to you."

"What? Where is Annie? Has something happened to her? Please tell me!" Maggie's voice rose with concern.

Principal Harris came out immediately and guided Mrs. Preston into her office.

"What is going on, Principal Harris?"

"I'm sorry, Mrs. Preston. Your husband came in earlier to pick up Annie. He said you were in a car accident and dying. He said you requested he pick up Annie and bring her to you right away."

"Well, as you can see, I am perfectly well. Why did you do that? You know that he is no longer on the pickup list for her. There is a reason for that."

"But you never said specifically that he could not pick her up. Why wouldn't you want him to be on the list? He is her father."

"Listen to me, Principal Harris. My husband is not to be on the list because he and I are in the process of getting a divorce. There could be a custody battle here. Besides, there is another reason which I do not care to share with you at this time."

"I see. Well, can't you go get her from him?"

"Things are not as simple as that. He is trying to take her away from me. I will have to call the police."

"The police? We don't want any trouble. We did nothing wrong here, Mrs. Preston."

"You most definitely did, Principal Harris. I did not put him on the list for pickup privileges. You cannot let someone pick up my child without my consent."

"I'm sorry this happened. Is there anything we can do to help you?"

"No, you already did enough, Principal Harris."

Maggie stormed out the door and raced home as she called the police on her cell. She explained the situation to them and then called her husband. She didn't expect him to answer.

"Hello."

"Nate, why did you pick up Annie? Don't you realize you are in trouble with the police? I just called them."

"I am her father, Maggie. You can't keep me away from Annie."

"Mommy, please come get me. I want you, Mommy!" Annie cried out loud enough for Maggie to hear her.

"I'm coming, sweetheart."

Nate ignored his daughter's pleas and continued, "Listen, Maggie. I just need to spend some time with her. I will bring her back in a few days."

"No, you can't do that! Didn't you realize her birthday is tomorrow! She is having a party and a friend over. She will be devastated if you do that."

"Her birthday? Oh, I forgot it's her birthday. That's okay. I will give her a party myself and take her out for ice cream. She will love it! Don't worry about her. I will take care of her, Maggie."

"No, no, you can't do this, Nate. The police will come to your house. They may be on their way there now."

"That's okay. I am not there anyway. They will never find me or Annie. You should have thought about this sooner. It's all your fault. You told me that we are finished. Well, maybe we are, but I am still Annie's father. She will stay with me. Goodbye, Maggie."

"No, no, Nate, please don't do this!" Maggie spoke into the empty phone. Tears were streaming down her face and blurring her vision as she ran home.

She ran through the foyer and game room and all the way up to the third floor. She went directly to Branyrd's door. But before she could open it Branyrd stepped out and took Maggie into her arms.

"What's happened, Maggie? Where's Annie?"

"She...she...wasn't at school! I spoke to Nate. He has her and is not bringing her back. He...has gone away somewhere. What am I going to do? How will I find her? I called the police but I don't think they are going to do anything. They said she is with her father. They can't do anything unless he harms her in some way."

"What does that mean? Harms her in some way? Aren't they supposed to help people? That doesn't sound like they are helping you." Branyrd whispered a few expletives once again and blessed herself quickly.

"What did you say, Branyrd?"

"Oh, nothing, Maggie. I am just as upset as you are. We will find Nate and bring Annie back. I will help you. Don't worry. Okay?"

"But how will you find him? I have no idea where he could be?"

"First, we must go to his apartment or house wherever that is. Do you have the address?"

"Yes, I know where it is. Annie and I lived there before. But he said he wasn't there."

"Well, do you believe him? He might just be saying that so you won't go there, Maggie."

"Yes, you are right. He would do that. Let's go. But we need transportation. It is too far to walk from here."

"Okay, let me get us some transportation from a friend. Wait a minute." Branyrd went inside her room and called out to Benedicto for help.

"I need you, Benedicto. Is this what you were talking about before? Something was going to happen?"

"Yes, this is it, Branyrd. You have to think it through and go find Annie. What do you need from me?"

"I thought you were all knowing, Benedicto? If you knew this was going to happen, then you know what I must do next."

"Yes, I was just testing you to see if you were aware of what you must do to rectify the situation. A taxi is outside waiting to take you to Nate's apartment. You must hurry."

"Can you come with me? Or at least be nearby in case I need your assistance?" Branyrd pleaded anxiously.

"I am always nearby, Branyrd, watching over you, little angel." He disappeared with his last word.

"I know you are, Benedicto. You better be close by. I have no idea what we will have to do against Nate. He could hurt both of us."

Branyrd came back out to Maggie and guided her downstairs to the taxi. "Let's go, Maggie. Give the driver the address quickly."

CHAPTER TWENTY

Maggie sighed heavily and gave Nate's address to the driver as she held tightly onto Branyrd's hands. "I can't believe this is happening, Branyrd. Thank you for helping me. I only hope we are not too late to find her."

"Don't worry, Maggie. We will find her. Nate will be punished for what he has done. He will not hurt her. He loves her, I'm sure. He is just angry with you for wanting to end your marriage. This is his way to get back at you."

"Yes, I think so too. But I am still worried about Annie. She sounded so frightened when I spoke with Nate. She yelled for me to come get her."

"Oh, I see. Of course, she didn't understand why he picked her up instead of you."

"Oh, Branyrd. What if he told her I was going to die like he told the school?"

"No, I don't think he would have said that. She heard your voice and knows that you are all right now. I think he probably told her that he was going to bring her home to you."

"I agree, Branyrd. Annie wouldn't have gone with him otherwise." Maggie looked up and said, "We're here, Branyrd."

Maggie paid the driver and told him to wait for them. "We'll be right back."

She knocked on Nate's door and waited with Branyrd by her side. There was no answer, so she knocked louder this time.

"Where is he? Maybe he was telling the truth and took Annie away."

"No, I think he is inside. Listen, I hear crying."

"Annie, are you in there? It's Mommy!"

The door opened and Nate stood there holding the door firmly. "What do you want, Maggie?"

"I want Annie. Let me take her home, Nate. You don't want to do this. She is innocent in all this. We need to talk about us. She shouldn't be in the middle."

"Mommy! Mommy, I want to go home!" Annie cried from somewhere inside the house.

"Let her go, Nate. Please listen to reason," Maggie begged.

Nate looked down at Branyrd. "Who is this, Maggie?"

"This is my friend, Branyrd. She is here to help me."

Branyrd smiled and put her hand out to Nate. "Hi, Nate."

Nate didn't know what to do. He wasn't expecting someone to be nice to him under the circumstances.

He shook Branyrd's hand and then smiled back at her saying, "Hi, Branyrd."

Maggie watched with her mouth opened wide in shock. What did Branyrd do to him to make him so complacent all of a sudden?

"Do you want to come in?" Nate stood aside and let Maggie and Branyrd in.

Maggie exchanged a perplexed look with Branyrd who shrugged her shoulders and followed her inside.

"Where's Annie, Nate?"

"I'll get her. Wait a minute." Nate left the living room and went into the bedroom in the back returning with a crying Annie.

"Mommy! Why did Daddy pick me up instead of you?"

"It's okay, Annie. I'm here now. We will be going home shortly."

"Hi Branyrd. I'm happy to see you. I can't wait for my party tomorrow. I'm glad you came to get me," Annie said, wiped her tears and stopped sniffling.

"I'm happy to see you too, Annie. Say goodbye to your daddy and we will leave. Okay?"

Annie turned to her father and hugged him and said, "Goodbye, Daddy."

Nate appeared to be in a trance as he hugged Annie and said goodbye back. He turned and left the living room and sat at the kitchen table.

"What's going on here, Branyrd? Did you do something to Nate to make him like this. I can't believe he is not fighting with me over Annie."

"Well, I think it is time to leave, Maggie. Get your school bag, Annie, and let's go quickly." Branyrd looked back at Benedicto who stood over Nate keeping him in the seat at the kitchen table, enabling them to leave.

Branyrd nodded at him and pushed Maggie and Annie out the door to the waiting taxi.

They all expelled a deep sigh of relief in the taxi as they drove away.

Inside Benedicto moved away from Nate as he came to his senses and looked around for Annie. He went throughout the house calling her name. "Where are you, Annie?" What happened? Where did she go? He shook his head to clear it and sighed. He couldn't remember what happened. All he could remember is that Maggie had come to the door asking for Annie then everything was a blur.

Benedicto was waiting outside for Branyrd when she came back to the Y. He nodded and smiled as she followed Annie and Maggie inside. Benedicto only appeared to Branyrd but could appear to others if needed.

Maggie turned to Branyrd and hugged her. "I don't believe what just happened. Did you do something to Nate? I have never seen him like that. He never would have let me take Annie without a fight."

"I didn't do anything, Maggie. But sometimes when we need help, HE is there to lend a hand like today. I did a lot of praying last night and every minute of the day today once I knew Annie was in danger."

"I don't always pray but maybe I should. I need to say a prayer of thanks for getting Annie back. Thank you, Branyrd, and your prayers for helping," Maggie said, feeling relieved and thankful.

"I'm sure HE knows how grateful you are, Maggie." Turning to Annie, Branyrd said, "How are you doing, Annie?"

"I'm better now that I am home with you and Mommy! Thank you for coming to pick me up from Daddy's. I don't think he wanted me to leave. But once you came, he let me go. I think he was being nice for a change."

"Yes, I think he was, Annie." Maggie said with a smile.

"Mommy, I'm hungry. I didn't get to eat anything while I was at Daddy's. He promised to give me some candy but then he forgot. He never has anything in his refrigerator either but beer. Can we go downstairs to eat?"

"Of course, Annie. Let's go see what they have for tonight."

Branyrd excused herself and said, "You two go and eat. I will join you later. I need to use the bathroom."

The angel waited for mother and daughter to leave so she could go back to her room and talk to Benedicto.

The Angel First Class on High was there when she opened the door.

"Well, that was something, Benedicto. I'm sure you did all that, right?"

"What makes you think I did anything, Branyrd?"

"I saw you as you kept Nate in his seat. You waited until we were gone before letting him get up, right?"

"Well, maybe I convinced him to stay put for a little while. He may try something again. So, you better warn Maggie and Annie to be alert. It is not over yet."

"I see."

"Maybe you did something to Nate when you shook his hand, Branyrd. Did you even think about that?"

"What could I have done? I don't have any magical powers, do I?"

Branyrd looked around but Benedicto was gone. He never answers my questions, she sighed heavily and left her room to join Maggie and Annie in the dining room.

CHAPTER TWENTY-ONE

Branyrd grabbed a cup of coffee which had become her favorite beverage on Earth. She sat down next to Maggie and Annie and sighed, contented.

Maggie smiled at Branyrd and said, "Thank you again, for all you did today. I don't think it would have gone smoothly without you being there. I just don't understand what happened to Nate," she whispered so Annie wouldn't hear.

"I don't have a clue either. I assure you. I had nothing to do with his complacency. I told you it was help from above."

"Of course. I know you believe that, Branyrd. But I …well, I just don't know. Nothing stops Nate from getting his way."

"Then you must be careful, Maggie. He may try something again," Branyrd warned.

"Yes, I know he will. He has to win every time. He will not be happy about this and whatever happened to him. The first thing I have to do is warn the school not to let him pick Annie up again for any reason. They don't seem to understand how important that is."

"That's a good idea, Maggie. Also, you might add that if Nate does try to pick Annie up that you must be notified at once."

"Yes, I will do that. He may try something again about my health being in danger. Well, if he tries that again, it will be his health that is in danger," Maggie declared with a frown creasing her brows.

"Oh, Maggie. You shouldn't say that. I know you don't mean it," Branyrd responded with a surprised look.

"Well, I guess I don't really mean that. I would never physically harm Nate even if I wanted to."

"That's good to hear, Maggie. I will help you again if you need me. I'm here for you."

"Thank you, Branyrd. I don't know what I did to deserve you as a friend in my life right now when I most needed you. But I am grateful for your friendship." Maggie wiped tears of relief away.

Branyrd blushed. "You're welcome, Maggie. I appreciate your friendship too. I don't have many real friends I can count on, either, so I understand how you feel."

Maggie noticed that Branyrd wasn't eating. "Aren't you ever hungry? I never see you eat anything. You only drink coffee."

"That's okay. I eat in my room most of the time, just a sandwich. I don't have much of an appetite."

Annie jumped in and exclaimed, "Branyrd loves ice cream! Don't you, Branyrd?"

"Yes...yes...I do, Annie. I love chocolate!"

"That's my favorite too, Branyrd. I can't wait for my birthday party tomorrow. Then I can have all the ice cream and cake that I can eat, right, Mommy?"

Maggie smiled and said, "Of course you can, Annie. As long as you don't get sick."

"You can have all you want too, Branyrd!" Annie exclaimed as she beamed at the angel.

"I'll do my best, Annie. I can't wait for your birthday either."

Unbeknownst to Annie, Branyrd had previously told all the women in the dining hall about Annie's birthday. They promised to pop over to see Annie, wish her a happy day and bring gifts the next day. They had become attached to the little girl who loved to play cards and Monopoly every chance she got.

***

Nate sat at his kitchen table and drank his third beer and snacked on chips. He kept shaking his head to try to clear it of this fog that appeared to be hanging over him. He couldn't figure out what had happened. How did Annie leave without him seeing her? He picked up his cell and called Maggie. He tapped his beer on the side of the table as he waited for her to answer.

Maggie stopped eating when she heard her phone ring. She looked at it and gasped, "It's Nate! What does he want?"

Branyrd guided Maggie away from the table so Annie couldn't hear. "You have to answer it, Maggie. He wants to know about Annie, I'm sure. He is probably confused about what happened."

"Right. That's it. I don't think he wants to cause any more trouble. I can only hope," she sighed.

She answered with a tentative, "Hi, Nate."

"What did you do to me, Maggie? Why did you take Annie?"

"I didn't do anything to you, Nate. Why do you think so?"

"I don't know. Something isn't right. I don't remember anything after you came to the door."

"That's not my fault. You let us in to take Annie home."

"I never would have done that…unless…something happened." Nate's voice was almost a whisper with an edge of fear evident there.

Branyrd watched Maggie's face and tried to tune into the conversation. She concentrated and heard Nate's voice change to a whisper.

Nate ended the call which surprised Maggie. She put her cell down and looked at Branyrd and shrugged her shoulders. "That was very strange. He was acting weird. Maybe something did happen to him. But I certainly didn't do anything. He seems to think I did."

Branyrd patted Maggie on the shoulder and said, "Don't worry about it. It's over now. Let's just be vigilant for what may come next."

Maggie looked at Branyrd with wide eyes. "What is going to happen next? What do you mean, Branyrd? Do you know something I don't know?"

"No, I didn't mean it to sound like that, so mysterious. I don't know anything except I don't trust Nate to not try something again."

"Yes, I agree. But he seemed to be so shocked over his own behavior. He blames me for that."

"Let's just concentrate on Annie and her party tomorrow. Don't give Nate another thought."

"But he may come to her party tomorrow, Branyrd. What do I do then?"

CHAPTER TWENTY-TWO

Annie was so excited when she woke up the next morning. She announced to her still groggy mother, "It's my birthday today, Mommy! I can't believe I am six today!"

"Yes, you are, sweetie!" Maggie rubbed her eyes and stretched to wake herself up. She knew that Annie wouldn't wait long to announce this to Branyrd too.

Go to the bathroom, wash up and get dressed, Annie. Then we can go downstairs. I'm sure Branyrd is still sleeping. You woke up a little early today. I know how excited you are. But you must let others sleep a little longer. Okay?"

"Okay, Mommy. But Branyrd will want to see me to wish me a 'happy birthday,' you know."

"Of course, she will. But we can see her soon when she is ready to come downstairs for her morning coffee."

Annie hung her head and followed her mother to the bathroom but looked back at Branyrd's door to see if it was opened.

Branyrd heard Annie's high-pitched voice announcing her birthday. The angel was doing her morning prayers and talking to Benedicto about the day ahead and filling in the LORD about everything he already knew.

Branyrd had explained what Nate had said to Maggie in their recent phone conversation. Benedicto nodded and smiled.

"I suspected he would be wondering what happened to him. Don't worry. I can erase the whole episode from his mind if you prefer."

"Would that be good to do, Benedicto? Then he wouldn't remember picking up Annie or her birthday today."

"I can be selective and erase only what needs to be erased."

"I see. Well, that's up to you and HIM. I don't have anything to do with that part of the mission. Do I?" Branyrd turned her head to give Benedicto a quizzical look.

Benedicto had disappeared right in front of her eyes.

"Oh, for shit's sake! Oops, sorry, LORD! I meant for goodness sakes. It just slipped out. I didn't mean that!"

"I'm sure you didn't, Branyrd!" the LORD responded and cut out with the slight edge of a chuckle.

"That's very strange. I swear (oops not really) that I heard a little titter from HIM. Maybe it was my imagination."

Branyrd changed her clothes and went to use the bathroom for the sake of appearances. She flushed the toilet, ran the faucet and headed downstairs for her morning coffee.

The dining hall was filled with the other inhabitants who were already enjoying their breakfasts.

Branyrd nodded to one and all and picked up her cup of coffee to bring back to the table next to Maggie and Annie.

Before the angel could sit down, Annie came rushing over to her and gave her a tight hug, nearly knocking the hot coffee out of her hand. Branyrd quickly put the coffee down on the table and hugged Annie back.

"Hey, birthday girl! It's your special day today!"

"Yes, I knew you would remember, Branyrd!" Annie smiled wider.

"Did you think I would forget my favorite six-year-old?" Branyrd gushed and returned the smile.

"I love you, Branyrd. I'm so glad you came to live here. You are my friend too, right?"

"Yes, I am your friend and your mother's, Annie." Branyrd tried to keep the tears from falling at these words. She didn't know if she would be around once her mission was completed. What would happen to Annie then? Would she forgive her for leaving?

The angel tried to wipe the unexpected tears away. She had never felt tears like this. For one thing, this was the first time she had a human form to feel the emotions that only humans felt. It was mind-boggling to an angel.

Maggie looked up and noticed Branyrd wiping her face. "Are you all right, Branyrd? What did Annie say to you? You look upset."

"Oh, she is just being an adorable and sweet little girl. She was happy that I remembered her birthday." Branyrd laughed. "It's hard to forget since that is all she has talked about for the past few days."

"Yes, I know. She woke me up extra early today to announce it to me."

"She is a lovely little girl, Maggie. You are so fortunate to have her. I know that your life with Nate wasn't always good but look what you have from it."

"I know, she is my whole world. I love her so much, Branyrd. I couldn't stand to lose her."

"You won't lose her, Maggie. I will watch over both of you to make sure nothing happens. Okay?"

"Thank you, Branyrd," Maggie said as she choked up.

"Boy, both of us are a little teary-eyed today on this special day," Branyrd announced with a smirk.

"I think we should show Annie happy faces for the rest of the day. No more tears. Okay?" Maggie said as she dabbed at the last vestiges of spent tears.

Annie looked at her mother and Branyrd and asked, "What's wrong, Mommy and Branyrd? Why are you sad? Today is a happy day."

"Yes, you are right, honey. Today is indeed a big day for one very special little girl who is now *six-years-old*!"

"Yay! I am six-years-old!" Annie announced for all to hear.

Clapping began all over the hall as everyone joined in and sang 'happy birthday.'

Annie took a bow and ran around and gave everyone a hug in appreciation.

Some of the women exchanged winks with Branyrd and Maggie and smiled. They would stop by later to drop off their presents to this special little girl who had captured their hearts.

CHAPTER TWENTY-THREE

Maggie arrived earlier for pickup at school so she could speak with the principal about her husband.

Principal Harris came out and ushered Maggie into her office. "What can I do for you, Mrs. Preston?" the principal asked tentatively after the last episode of pickup.

"I would like to have this statement put on my daughter's record about pickup." Maggie handed the handwritten statement about her husband not being allowed to pick up Annie for any reason and for her to be informed if he ever tried again.

"Yes, I will put this on her record right away, Mrs. Preston. We are so sorry for any confusion about the previous pickup.

I hope all is well with you and Annie since then. You were quite upset."

"Yes, I was quite upset. I had a reason to be, Principal Harris. I would appreciate it if you would call me if Mr. Preston comes in here and tries to pick up Annie again."

"Of course, I will call you personally, Mrs. Preston. I hope you have a good day. I need to make sure my secretary records this right away. Thank you for coming in to report this."

Maggie shook Principal Harris's hand and left the room to wait outside with the other mothers for her daughter to appear.

Annie was one of the first to come out to meet her mother escorted by Principal Harris. Maggie took charge of Annie and thanked the principal and walked away holding protectively onto Annie's little hand.

Maggie listened with half an ear as Annie described her day in school and her new friend, Deidra. "She is coming over soon, Mommy. Her mother is driving her over. I am so excited to see my cake and have some ice cream with Deidra and you and Branyrd."

***

While Maggie was at pickup, Branyrd got the hall decorated with balloons of all colors but mostly pink and purple, Annie's favorite colors. Benedicto blew them up for Branyrd when she became exhausted after working on one. Branyrd had help from the other occupants of the YMCA who

140

brought more decorations they had to add to make it even more festive.

Branyrd spied Maggie and Annie coming up the street and announced, "Hide, everyone. They're coming!"

Annie walked in ahead of her mother and screamed out loud when she saw all the balloons and crepe paper all over the hall. "Wow! I love it! Who did this?" She looked around, but no one was there.

A second later, the hall broke out with "Surprise, Annie! Happy Birthday!" as everyone jumped out from their hiding places.

"Oh, thank you so much, everyone! Did you do this, Branyrd?"

One woman stepped forward, "Yes, she did. She asked us to stop by to see you. Of course, we would have come anyway without her permission."

"Everyone helped to make this day special for you, Annie," Branyrd announced.

"Thank you, everyone. I love the balloons. They are my favorite colors. I can't wait for Deidra to see this too! She will love it!"

Annie hugged Branyrd first and then went down the line to each and every woman who stood there with beaming faces.

The woman who spoke up before said, "Well, we left our presents on the table for you Annie. We will stop by later to see if you liked them. You need time with your family and friend. See you later. We're so happy you liked the decorations. Have fun at your party!"

Annie smiled and waved and threw kisses to the ladies before turning back to look at the table laden with several presents and wrapped with large bows.

"Wow, look at all the presents! It looks like I have a lot of friends who came to my party."

"Yes, you do have a lot of friends. All the ladies here love you, Annie. You must thank each and every one of them later after you open their presents. You are one lucky little girl," Maggie announced as she hugged her daughter who was bouncing around in joy.

Maggie smiled with tears in her eyes at Branyrd. She mouthed, 'thank you' to the angel.

The angel nodded with misty eyes also. She mouthed back, 'you're welcome.'

A short time later Deidra showed up with her mother. She raced into the hall once she spotted the decorations. Annie was right there to greet her with a happy face.

Deidra's mother greeted Maggie and said she would be back in a few hours for her daughter. "Here's my number in case I need to be back sooner to pick up Deidra."

"No problem. Thank you for bringing her," Maggie smiled and walked Deidra's mother to the door.

Deidra announced in a squeaky, excited voice, "I love the decorations, Annie! They are beautiful! You have the biggest room I have ever seen for a party! I can't wait to begin having fun!"

"Yeah, I love the decorations too, Deidra. All my friends here put them up. Here's my friend, Branyrd. She is the best."

Branyrd greeted Deidra and said, "It's so nice to meet Annie's new friend. Would you like to have a drink and play some games, Deidra?"

"Yes! What are we going to play?" Deidra looked at Annie for an answer.

Annie shrugged her shoulders. "I didn't plan anything." She looked at Branyrd for an answer to this question. "What are we going to play, Branyrd?"

"Well, there are all kinds of card games and board games to play. Let's go pick out what you want to do."

Maggie stepped forward and offered, "How about pin the tail on the donkey?"

Both girls yelled out at the same time, "Yes!!"

Maggie set up the game, helped the girls with the masks and turned them around in a circle. They giggled and walked toward what they thought was the donkey to pin the tail.

Branyrd had never seen this game before and laughed along with the girls. She tried to give them hints where to go to be successful in pinning the tail on the wall instead of on some unsuspecting passerby.

While this was going on, Branyrd noticed Nate staring through the window of the hall at them.

Maggie noticed this at the same time and hurried over. She whispered to Branyrd, "What are we going to do? We can't let him in. He might try to disrupt the party."

"I know. Let me talk to him. I will let him know that he can only come in if he behaves himself."

"Okay," Maggie said anxiously.

Branyrd opened the door and beckoned Nate closer so she could talk to him quietly. "You are not allowed to come in if you are going to cause any trouble. This is a special day for your daughter. You will not do anything to get in the way of her having fun. Do you understand, Nate?"

Nate looked at Branyrd with disbelief. "Who do you think you are, talking to me like that? Annie is my daughter. What is she to you? I don't even know who you are. Get out of my way. I want to wish my daughter a happy birthday."

"Did you bring her a present?" Branyrd asked, looking at Nate's empty hands.

"I...um...I forgot to bring it."

"Well, you are not allowed in without a present. When you have one, come back."

Branyrd closed and locked the door behind her leaving Nate looking confused and frustrated at this little person who just scolded him. He shook his head and walked away.

Maggie hurried over to talk to Branyrd. "What did you say to him to make him go away?"

"Well, I told him he had to behave and not disrupt the party. I also said he could not come in without a present."

"That was clever, Branyrd. I would never have thought of that," Maggie guffawed.

"He will be back, hopefully with a present.," Branyrd smirked with satisfaction.

The girls hadn't noticed Nate was there. They were too busy playing games and giggling themselves silly.

***

Branyrd watched Nate walk away until he was out of sight.

CHAPTER TWENTY-FOUR

Maggie kept looking out the window expecting Nate to come back. She tried to enjoy watching her daughter play different games with her friend. She was too nervous to concentrate on anything but her husband's possible reappearance.

Branyrd came up behind Maggie and touched her elbow causing Maggie to jump. "Oh, sorry. I didn't mean to startle you. Are you okay, Maggie? Please don't worry about Nate. If he comes back, I will handle him. Go play with your daughter. She needs her mother to be happy on her special day."

Maggie nodded and joined Annie and Deidra as they played card games. Maggie watched the girls and relaxed. Annie smiled at her mother and said, "Thank you, Mommy, for this fun party! Can we do this again next year?"

"We'll see, Annie. We may not be living here. We'll have to see. Okay, sweetheart?"

"Okay, Mommy. But Deidra will come to my party next year, won't you, Deidra?"

Deidra smiled and said, "Of course I will come. You better come to my party in three months too, Annie. Maybe I can have it here like you did. This is so much fun!"

The girls tired after a while with the card game and announced, "Can we have cake and ice cream now?"

Maggie answered after glancing toward the window again, "Yes, I think it is time for some. Then you can open your presents."

"Yay! Presents! I can't wait to see what you got me, Deidra, and also everyone else. Did you see all my presents on the table?"

"Yes, I hope you like my present. I can't wait to see what else you got in those big boxes," Deidra exclaimed in wide-eyed wonder.

***

In another part of the neighborhood, Nate went to a toy store to try to find a present for his daughter. He couldn't believe the nerve of that little woman telling him to do this. He didn't believe either, that here he was doing just what she told him to do. He did want to give Annie a present for her birthday. What kind of father would he be if he didn't?

147

As he was entering the store a gang of men walked by and stopped him from going in. "Where are you going, Nate?"

Nate looked at the man who spoke, and in a shaky voice he said, "Oh, Mitch. I'm going to buy my daughter a present for her birthday."

"Well, look at that, guys. Nate is getting soft in his old age. He wants to buy his daughter a present. How sweet!"

"Listen Mitch. I don't want any trouble. Let me do this and leave me alone."

"Leave you alone? You owe me for the smack I gave you last week. I told you if you didn't pay me back within a few days you were dead. Did you forget that?"

"No, I didn't. But I don't have the money yet. I will get it. I plan to get it from my wife. She owes me big time."

"Is that right? Why, does she owe you big time? Did you give her something? I know what you have there in your pants is not big." Mitch laughed and the rest of his gang joined in.

"Very funny, Mitch. I don't have time for this. I promise to get you the money. I need more time."

"I thought you wanted to be part of this gang. But you have to pass our initiation first. If you pass it then you won't have to pay up this time."

"What initiation?" Nate's curiosity was piqued when he heard he wouldn't have to pay up for the smack. "What do I have to do?"

"Well, come with us and I will tell you." Mitch led Nate away from the store.

***

Back at Annie's party everyone was having cake and ice cream after Annie made a wish and blew out her candles. She was having her second helping of chocolate ice cream along with Branyrd.

Maggie eyed the scoop of ice cream and watched her daughter dive in. She was worried that Annie was overdoing it and would suffer later. She edged closer to Annie and whispered in her ear, "Honey, I think you have had enough. Why don't we save some for tomorrow. Okay? It's time to open your presents anyway."

The mention of presents did it and Annie put down her spoon and ran over to the table laden with gifts. She sat down and pulled the first present over to her.

Deidra smiled brightly and announced, "That's my present, Annie. I hope you like it!"

Annie opened it with gusto, tearing the paper to shreds as she slipped out the box. "Wow! I love it, Deidra! I've always wanted a yoyo, and it's purple with sparkles! I will have to learn how to use it. Can you teach me?"

"Well, I have one but I don't know how to do it very well. We can learn together. Okay?"

"Okay. That sounds good. Thank you, Deidra."

Soon the mound of presents was opened and the pile of paper was all over the floor at Annie's feet. Branyrd and the other women who had come back to see Annie open them, helped to clean up the mess.

Annie thanked everyone for all the great presents and left the room to take Deidra back to her bedroom to practice yoyoing. Annie now had a few more board games, cards, and pretty outfits from her friends which she brought back to her room with Deidra's help.

Maggie whispered to Branyrd. I wonder why Nate didn't come back? You told him to go get a present for Annie."

"Yes, I did. That was just to get him to leave. I didn't know if he would do it or not. Maybe that is where he is. Don't think about it. He must have changed his mind about it and gone home," Branyrd surmised.

"I don't want him to come back but Annie will wonder why her father didn't even give her a present on her birthday."

"I think she is too busy with her friend right now. She may realize it tomorrow. Then you will have to talk to her about this situation of your divorce."

"What am I going to do? How will Annie take it? I hope she won't be angry with me."

Branyrd took Maggie's hand and squeezed it. "I don't think she will. Do you remember the look on her face when we brought her out of his apartment? She was relieved."

"Yes, I saw that too. I think she was frightened by her father's irrational behavior at first and then relieved when he let her go."

"She will be confused. I'm sure when it is all over, you may have to give Nate visitation rights." Branyrd had discussed this with Benedicto who informed her of the process of a divorce.

"I may not have to if there is evidence of abuse. I should have gone to the hospital when he hit me. That would be proof of his violent nature."

"Yes, but now it is too late to worry about, Maggie. The best thing you can do is hire a lawyer and get things rolling. You should document everything, though, just the same."

Maggie looked at Branyrd and smiled, "Look who knows so much about divorce all of a sudden. Where did you learn your facts?"

Branyrd blushed and said, "I have a friend who knows about these things. In fact, he knows about everything."

"Really? I would like to have a friend like that. Who is he? Boyfriend?"

"Oh no, Maggie. I don't have a boyfriend. It is not…umm, not a boyfriend, just a friend."

Maggie looked more closely at Branyrd as her face flushed and she wouldn't look Maggie in the eye. Something was strange there. Who was this guy?

"I'm going to get a cup of coffee, Maggie. Do you want one?" Branyrd had to get away from Maggie's stare that felt like Maggie was seeing right through the angel's deceptions.

"Sure. I'll come with you. I think we should talk some more about this guy, Branyrd."

CHAPTER TWENTY-FIVE

"Why are you doing this to me?" Nate said as he tried to take a breath. His nose was broken and his left eye almost closed. The White Stag Gang had taken him to their warehouse and beaten him, each taking a swing at him.

The leader, Mitch, answered after kicking Nate in the kidneys once again. "This is your initiation, Nate. Didn't you realize that?"

"What kind of initiation is this?" Nate tried to wipe his nose on his sleeve but with his hands tied behind his back it wasn't easy to do. He let the blood drip down onto his chest instead.

"This is only part of your initiation, Nate. The second part is for you to steal some money from a store. Your choice of the store."

Nate tried to laugh but it hurt too much everywhere. "How am I to do that? Look at me! I am a mess. I can't go into a store like this!"

"That is up to you to figure out, Nate. You have three days to get this done. I expect you to have at least two hundred dollars to give me at that time."

"But...I..." Nate looked around and noticed they had all disappeared. He worked at his ties until he could feel them loosen. He didn't stop wiggling around until the restraints were off completely. He freed his legs and left the building after peeking out to see if the men were really gone.

He hurried home and washed and bandaged his face. He couldn't do anything about his ribs. They ached and his side was all bruised from the many kicks he received. He probably had a couple of broken ribs and a damaged kidney to boot. He knew he couldn't go to the hospital. There would be too many questions that he couldn't answer.

Nate couldn't believe he had put himself in this predicament. What was wrong with him? He knew he shouldn't have gotten the smack from the White Stag Gang. He knew they were bad news. He should have listened to Maggie. She told him not to trust Mitch and his gang.

He lay down to rest after tossing back a few extra strength pain killers with a bottle of beer. Before he knew it, he was fast asleep.

When he woke up it was 8:00 in the morning. He groaned as he tried to move off the couch. He couldn't believe what the Gang had done to him. He should never have gone with them willingly. He could have put up a fight and maybe someone would have noticed and helped him to get away.

He got another beer and drank that down to deaden the pain. He couldn't believe that he ached in so many places at one time. He felt hungry but was afraid to eat anything for fear of getting sick. The idea of regurgitating his beers was too much to think about and would hurt like hell. He grabbed a bag of chips to munch on and curtail his hunger for the time being.

He looked at the mail that was on his kitchen table. He hadn't opened it yet. He knew most of it was bills that he couldn't pay. What was he going to do? How was he going to get money to pay Mitch. He didn't want to rob a store. That would only put him back in jail. He had already gone that route and couldn't go back.

His phone rang and he moaned and pulled himself up by the table to reach it on the wall. He didn't recognize the number but answered it anyway.

"Hello. Who is this?" He listened for a few minutes to a voice that was not familiar to him.

"Is this Nate Preston?"

"Yes. Who is this?"

"This is a warning. You must change your ways. You will never see your daughter like this."

"What? Who is this? Who do you think you are?"

There was silence in his ear as he looked at the phone and put it on the table. He had no idea who that was. Who would say that to him? Could it be his wife who had someone call to warn him? He knew she was in the process of separating from him and would most likely file for a divorce. He would never see Annie again if that happened.

"I have to do something. I need help. Please, someone help me!" Nate cried out in despair.

A light appeared in the doorway as an enormous man stepped into the room. Nate had never seen this huge man before. He was dressed like he lived around here but his features were not like anyone he had ever seen before. His face looked as if it were carved in stone and perfect in every way.

Nate felt embarrassed by the fact that he actually thought the man was quite handsome with dark hair and perfect features. His body was well muscled and his tee-shirt pulled across his chest showing the definition of each muscle. The man stood nearly eight feet tall or more and looked down on him with menacing eyes.

Nate felt tongue-tied and just stared up at the imposing figure in front of him. He was at a loss as to what to say even if he could talk.

The figure came closer to Nate who shivered and curled up into a ball on the chair to get away from the visitor.

"Nate, I am Benedicto. I heard your plea for help. Are you ready to make amends?"

"What do you mean you heard my plea for help?" Nate was clearly confused and shook his head back and forth and dropped his head onto his hands.

"You need to change your ways," the man stated.

"You are the one who called a little while ago, aren't you? I recognize your voice. How did you hear me say that I needed help?"

"We hear everything you say and see everything you do."

"What? I don't understand." Nate was feeling more frightened by the second and didn't know what to do or where to go.

The huge man continued to stare at him.

"What do you want from me? I don't have any money. Just leave me alone. I don't need your help whoever you are. I don't understand any of this."

"You need to change your ways. If you want any help at all, that is what you must do."

"What? Change my ways? Look at me! I am a mess. I know I have done some bad things in my day. But I don't know how else to live. I am at a loss. I can't keep a job and no one wants to help me. My wife is separating from me and will soon file for a divorce. I will never see my daughter. I should just kill myself and end it once and for all."

"NO!" the man yelled.

His voice was so loud that Nate's ears felt as if they would burst. Nate closed his eyes and covered his ears to prevent them from erupting. When the sound dissipated, he opened his eyes but the man was gone.

Nate felt cold and shivered from shock not only from his injuries but from the unexpected visitor. No one would believe him if he told them this man had come there. He had no idea where the man came from and how he knew what he had said about needing help.

He went into the bathroom and looked in the mirror. What he saw there surprised him. His face was nearly back to normal, his nose was straight and his eyes were completely open. He still felt a little soreness in his chest and abdomen but was feeling a lot better. What happened? How did this come about? Did the man do this? How?

Nate was about to reach for another beer but instead he brewed a strong cup of coffee and made himself an egg and toast. He sat down to eat for the first time in a long while. He had been living on beer and snacks mostly. He suddenly felt as if he had a purpose and a reason to live.

He left the house and returned to the toy store to pick out a gift for his daughter. He had to make amends with her first of all. Then he would ask Maggie for his forgiveness. He knew she may never give it but he had to try.

Nate picked out a doll that had the same blonde hair color as his Annie. The doll had the same blue eyes and wore a pink dress, Annie's favorite color. He paid the clerk and asked for it to be wrapped if possible. The woman happily did that and smiled at him.

He couldn't believe that someone actually smiled at him. He felt his mouth forming into a smile, too, as he thanked the woman and went out the door with his package under his arm.

He hurried along the way to the YWCA to give Annie the present. He hoped she would like it and forgive him for frightening her about her mother being in an accident when he had picked her up. But he couldn't remember if he had told her that or not.

He stood outside the Y and waited for someone to open the door. The man at the desk talked to him through the intercom. "Who are you? Are you visiting someone?"

"Yes, I am here to see my daughter, Annie Preston. Yesterday was her birthday. I have a present for her."

The man replied, "Wait a minute. I need to get permission for you to enter from Mrs. Preston."

Nate bounced back and forth from one foot to another as he waited. He watched the man talk to someone on a phone and then put the phone down and come toward the door.

The man opened the door and told Nate, "Take a seat. Mrs. Preston will be right down."

"Thank you." Nate was relieved that at least he got inside and would explain to Maggie that he was sorry.

Maggie discussed Nate's visit with Branyrd before she went down to see him. Branyrd stayed upstairs with Annie while Maggie did this.

"Nate, what are you doing here?"

Nate jumped up at the sight of his wife. "I have a present for Annie. I'm sorry about everything, Maggie. Can you forgive me? I just want to see Annie."

"I don't know if she wants to see you after what you did."

"I know. But I need to apologize for everything. I am trying to change, Maggie. Can't you see that? I want to change. I know I have not been a good person to either of you. Please let me see Annie for just a minute. I want her to open her present."

Nate sat back down and sighed. He flinched when his ribs sent a pain through him that was evidenced in his face.

"What's wrong, Nate? Are you in pain?" Maggie asked as she looked at his face all scrunched up.

"I…never mind. I don't want to bother you. Can you give Annie this present for me? Tell her I love her and that I'm sorry."

Maggie saw that something was wrong with Nate and said, "Wait here. I will get her."

She raced back upstairs and a few minutes later returned with Annie.

"Hi Daddy. Mommy said you wanted to see me."

"Yes, sweetheart. I want to apologize for my terrible behavior the other day and give you a birthday present." He handed her the present and turned to go.

"Wait, Daddy. Aren't you going to wait until I open it?" Annie said sweetly, surprised her father had remembered to give her a present.

"Okay. Open it. I'll wait," he sighed as he looked at his wife for approval.

Maggie nodded at Nate and said, "Yes, Annie, open up your present. I'm sure your daddy wants to see if you like it."

Annie tore the paper in shreds in her excitement to see what he had brought her. She couldn't remember her daddy giving her a present before. It was always her mother who did that.

She gasped in surprise as she looked inside and saw the doll who looked a lot like her with its blonde hair and blue eyes.

Annie rushed over to her father and gave him a tight hug. "Thank you so much, Daddy. I love her! I will call her Leana." She smiled and hugged her dolly close to her chest as she ran upstairs to show Branyrd her latest present.

Nate turned and headed toward the door but Maggie's voice stopped him. "Wait, Nate. I want to thank you, too, for doing this. You made Annie happy for...umm. Thank you."

"I know what you were going to say, Maggie. For once I made her happy and did something right. I'm really trying. Something strange happened to me. I was sitting down feeling sorry for myself after the beat..."

"What, Nate? After what? I know something happened to you. I can see it in the way you hold your side. You are injured. Who did this to you?"

"It's nothing, Maggie. I should have listened to you long ago about getting involved with Mitch and the White Stag Gang."

"Oh, Nate. You need to get away from them once and for all!" Maggie exclaimed.

"Yes, I am doing that, Maggie. Now I need to tell you something that happened to me. Something that was very strange. You may not believe me though."

"Try me, Nate. I have also experienced some strange things lately."

Maggie's eye grew wide as she listened to Nate explain about the giant man who had visited him.

CHAPTER TWENTY-SIX

Branyrd was talking to Benedicto when she heard a small knock on her door. She opened the door to see an excited and flushed Annie standing there holding out a doll.

"Well, what is this, Annie?"

"Look what my daddy just gave me for my birthday. Isn't she beautiful? I named her Leana. Daddy actually smiled at me. I think he is happier now than before."

"She is beautiful, Annie. In fact, she looks a lot like you. I bet your daddy was glad that he made you happy with his gift." Branyrd looked around but Benedicto was nowhere in sight. She wondered if he had anything to do with this gift.

Annie came in and sat on Branyrd's bed and talked non-stop about her dolly and how she couldn't wait to show Leana to her friend Deidra.

Branyrd let her go on and just listened. She was relieved to see how happy Annie was about her father for a change.

The angel was about to ask if Annie wanted to get something to eat since it was dinner time when she heard Maggie's voice out in the hall.

"Annie. Where are you, sweetie?"

Branyrd opened her door and welcomed Maggie inside. Maggie noticed her daughter sitting on Branyrd's bed talking to her doll and sighed, "I see she is boring you with her new present too, Branyrd. Sorry about that. It's good to see her so happy with her father. He finally did something right. He told me about a strange thing that happened to him. I didn't know whether to believe him or not. But some strange things have happened lately, so I guess anything is possible. Can we go outside in the hall so I can share something with you, Branyrd? I don't want Annie to hear this."

"Of course. Annie, you stay here, honey. We will be right back," Maggie announced.

Branyrd listened while Maggie told her about the man who appeared to Nate and what he said about Nate changing his ways.

"That is a little strange. Does he know who this man is?" Branyrd asked, knowing well who it was.

"No. Nate said he never saw him before. It freaked him out a little though. Nate also said that he had been beaten by the White Stag Gang because he owed them money. I told Nate not to get mixed up with them. They are nothing but trouble. But after the man left, his injuries were not as severe and he felt a lot better. That reminds me of when you touched me and my injuries healed. Does that mean the man was an…um…an angel? Are you an angel too, Branyrd?"

The angel's eyes widened at the name of the White Stag Gang. She composed herself and giggled nervously but answered, "Oh, no. I don't think so. I told you everything that happens is because of HIM. I cannot heal people. You have to believe in HIM and all good things will come to pass."

"But you sound and act like a spiritual being, Branyrd. I have never heard you say anything bad about anyone. You are too good."

"Well, I am not perfect. I assure you, Maggie. But thank you for the compliments. I have to watch my language. I have been told to do that often enough."

"Really? I don't believe that, Branyrd."

"I can't say anything more about that or…well. Just believe me. Okay? Now what about Nate? Is he okay after the beating?"

"He seems to be a little sore but better, he said."

"Maggie, do you know who the White Stag Gang are?"

"All I know is that they are bad news. They are known to sell drugs to kids on the street. I think Nate took some from them to sell and now can't pay them back. He is in trouble if he doesn't pay them within three days, he said. I don't know what possessed him to do that."

"Three days? What will they do if he doesn't make the payment?"

"Nate said they would kill him or maybe go after Annie and I. I can't believe that but I am frightened about the idea of someone wanting to harm my daughter. Do you think that I should go to the police?"

Branyrd listened to Benedicto in her head telling her what to say. She responded, "No, don't do that yet. I will see what I can do to help."

"You can't get involved, Branyrd! What can you do to stop them? They are dangerous men, Nate told me. They have no conscience about hurting children."

"Let me think this over, Maggie. Let's take Annie down for dinner. I could use a cup of coffee. How about you?"

"Sure." Maggie looked at Branyrd and sighed, not sure what Branyrd was going to do.

Annie skipped ahead of them holding onto her new doll. She couldn't take her eyes off of it for a moment. But in order to eat she had to put it down on the table where Branyrd could watch over it for her.

With a plate full of food, Annie came back to the table. "Thank you, Branyrd, for taking care of my dolly. I got a sandwich for her, too, in case she's hungry." Annie pretended to feed the doll and chewed, making the sounds for her.

Maggie whispered to Branyrd, "Have your figured out what we can do?"

"I am working on it. I will have my friend help me."

"Who is this friend you keep talking about? You said he knows a lot about everything. Right?"

"Yes, I guess he does. He can do just about anything. He will know what to do about Nate."

Maggie wore a puzzled expression as she observed Branyrd, who was deep in thought. "What do you think this friend of yours can do to help Nate? I hope he isn't like one of the White Stag Gang."

"No, he certainly is nothing like the Gang. I don't know yet what he will do but I'm sure he will come up with something that will keep Nate and both of you safe from harm."

"I hope so. In the meantime, I will keep Annie home for a day or two until we figure this all out."

"Good idea, Maggie. I will get him to work on it right away. I don't want Annie to miss too much school."

"It's only kindergarten. I don't think she will miss much. I will take some time off work too. I'll tell my boss that Annie is sick and I have to stay home with her."

"If you can't get time off, Maggie, I can stay with her and keep her safe. I will read stories to her and have her practice her alphabet and numbers so she won't forget them."

"You would do that, Branyrd? Wow, you really are an angel." Maggie laughed and hugged Branyrd.

"Okay? It's settled. You will go to work and I will stay with Annie. I don't think she is ready to leave her dolly to go to school anyway," Branyrd announced.

"I think you may be right, Branyrd," Maggie giggled as she looked at her daughter feeding herself and her doll.

Branyrd nodded her head to Maggie and said, "I will do all I can to keep you both safe."

Maggie smiled and squeezed Branyrd's hand with gratitude and relief.

Branyrd went into full planning-mode with Benedicto as she sipped her coffee. He shared his plans with her to an extent and told her to keep Annie inside until he said otherwise.

She responded in her mind, "I will do all I can, Benedicto."

CHAPTER TWENTY-SEVEN

Nate went home feeling good about how Annie responded to his gift. He, for once, did a good deed and thought of someone else rather than himself.

He opened the door to his apartment and rummaged around for something to eat. All he had in his refrigerator was some beer and spoiled milk. He had eaten the last egg and slice of bread. He sat down to make a list of what he would need and went back out.

While he was at the supermarket, he filled his cart but kept a tally of how much he was spending. He didn't have much in his pocket and he wasn't sure his card would take another jolt of spending.

Nate was relieved to get out of the store with a little money left over in his pocket for emergencies until he could get another job. He couldn't sell any more drugs. His parole officer was keeping a close eye on him. One wrong turn and he would be back in prison for a very long time. He was fortunate the last time he got caught stealing he only had to do six months' time.

Nate didn't see the White Stag Gang following him to his car since he was too involved with daydreaming about his daughter and the beautiful smile that lit up her face when she looked at her new doll.

Mitch poked Nate in the back which caused him to jump in alarm and nearly knock over his cart.

"What do you want, Mitch? Didn't you beat me enough already? I haven't had time to get the money. Don't you understand? If you keep hurting me, I will never be able to get a job."

"I'm keeping an eye on you, Nate. I don't trust you. But it looks like you are almost healed. Maybe you need another reminder."

"No, I don't. Now leave me alone." Nate opened his trunk, loaded his groceries and didn't look back at the glare of Mitch's eyes as he pulled out of the parking lot and headed home.

Nate sat down to eat his first meal, in, he didn't know how long. Well, that is not counting the egg and toast he had for breakfast. He had been mostly existing on beer and snacks. Both of those items were taking a toll on his health. He felt like crap and looked like it too. No wonder his wife and child left him and didn't want anything to do with him. But he knew it was more than that. He had struck his wife on more than one occasion. He couldn't control his temper especially when he was under the influence of drugs or booze.

He looked around and shivered. It was as if someone was watching him. Was it that giant of a man again? What was he anyway? Some kind of angel or something else?

He finished his sandwich and coffee and had an apple for dessert. The feeling that he was being watched did not go away. There was a nagging feeling deep inside him that told him he had to change and be a better husband and father. But was it too late?

***

Maggie cleared the two tables at the diner where she worked. She sprayed the table with cleaner and scrubbed it until it shined. It felt cathartic for her to do this. It was as if she was scrubbing her life clean of Nate.

She was grateful for her new friend's help. Branyrd was truly sent from Heaven, she mused and chuckled to herself. Annie kept telling her that Branyrd was a real angel who didn't have wings yet. Her daughter had such an imagination. But she was thinking along the same lines about everything good that had happened lately since Branyrd came into their lives.

Annie was such a special child. Maggie worried constantly about her. She vowed she would do all she could to keep her safe and work hard to get them a home. She had been saving up her paychecks since she began working before Annie was born at odd jobs. There still wasn't enough for a down payment on a house. She would have to get a raise or find a better paying job. She would have to settle, in the meantime, for renting an apartment or condo for her and Annie until she could save up enough eventually for a house.

She hadn't trusted Nate to provide for her and Annie especially after he was arrested for robbery and went away for six months.

Now she was extra careful and didn't spend money on anything other than their rent and expenses at the YWCA and things for Annie for school. She had made some clothes for her daughter to help defer that expense. But lately she had been too busy working to find time to sew again. Besides, her sewing machine was at the apartment with Nate. She would have to go there and get it.

Maggie was so busy inside her head musing over everything, that she didn't hear her boss calling her.

"Maggie? Girl, are you deaf or something? I need this table cleared and there are people waiting to sit down. Hurry up."

"Oh sorry, Tracy. I didn't hear you. There is too much in my head, I guess."

"Are you okay? Did Annie have a good birthday?"

Maggie began clearing the table and giving it a scrub as she conversed with her boss. "Yes, to both of your questions."

She sat the people down at the cleared table and gave them menus as she smiled and welcomed them to Tracy's Diner. She placed glasses of water in front of them and left to give them time to choose their lunch selections.

The diner was busier than ever which Maggie liked. It made the time fly by. Before she knew it, it was time for her dinner break. Afterward, she quickly went back to work. She had promised to work an extra shift since she had taken time off for Annie's party. Now she just had to find a sitter for Annie for the extra shifts and for weekends. She thought of Branyrd and how kind she had been to them. Maggie couldn't keep on taking advantage of Branyrd and depend on her to take care of Annie. Maggie was also worried about her husband and had to make sure that Nate stayed away from them. She had to get a divorce and put him out of their life for good.

But first, she needed to get some things out of the apartment like her sewing machine and the rest of her and Annie's clothes. She had rushed out of there without much previously.

The dinner crowd was slowing down so she took a moment to call Branyrd to check on Annie.

"Hi, Branyrd. How are you and Annie doing?"

"We're doing school work. Annie loves to play school. Who would have thought?" Branyrd giggled.

"Yes, she loves to play anything that is make believe. She likes that better than school itself."

Branyrd could tell by Maggie's tone something was up. "Are you okay, Maggie? Is there anything I can do for you?"

"Umm, well, I do need to pick up some things from Nate's apartment. I will call him first to make sure he isn't home."

"Are you sure that is a good idea, Maggie. What if he comes home when you are there? You could be in danger," Branyrd stressed.

"I will be careful and do it quickly. Don't worry. Can you stay with Annie and bring her down for dinner? I will be home as soon as I can."

"Of course, Maggie. Annie already ate and is now having an ice cream. I'm having one too. Can't expect her to eat one alone," Branyrd guffawed.

"That's good. As long as Annie is eating ice cream, she won't miss me. Thank you so much, Branyrd, for all that you do for Annie and me. I don't know what we would do without you."

"My pleasure, Maggie. Call me when you are all done at the apartment and on your way home. I will worry otherwise."

"I will, Branyrd. Thank you again. See you both soon." Maggie hung up and finished up with her last-minute clearing and resetting the tables for the next day. She said goodbye to her boss and headed over to Nate's in her rented car as she called his number again. There was no answer so she continued on her way.

What she didn't notice was a dark sedan following her.

CHAPTER TWENTY-EIGHT

The White Stag Gang didn't like the way Nate was ignoring them. The members of the Gang met in their warehouse to plan their next move. They had lost money when Nate refused to sell drugs for them again. Nate also owed them some back pay from the unsold drugs he still had.

The Gang couldn't afford Nate snitching on them about the drugs they sold around town. The police were closing in on some of the other gangs now. Mitch knew that he had to keep his sales quiet for a little longer. He gathered his men together to tell them what he wanted them to do.

Mitch sent two of his men to Tracy's Diner with this message, "You need to keep an eye on Nate's wife, Maggie. She works at the diner. I want to know what she is doing at all times and where she is going. It may lead us to Nate. He is up to something. I can feel it. Keep me informed what you find."

The two Gang members nodded, went out to one of the cars and headed over to the diner.

Mitch sent two more members to Nate's apartment. "You two, go to Nate's apartment and keep an eye on him. I want to know where he is going and when. Don't let him see you. Phone me with anything that seems out of the ordinary."

"Yes, Boss," both men responded in tandem.

The two men outside the diner watched as Maggie drove away in an older model car. They followed at a safe distance and slowed down if they got too close to her.

Maggie pulled up in front of Nate's apartment and called him one more time to ensure he wasn't there. No answer. She used her key to open the door and went to the bedroom she had once shared with Nate. She pulled out all her clothes from the closet and drawers. She put everything into a plastic bag she found under the sink. She ignored the mess in the kitchen, the sink full of dirty dishes, and the living room with newspapers and empty bottles of beer all over the table.

Next, she went to Annie's room and cleaned out her closet and drawers. She put all Annie's clothes, toys and books into a second bag and dragged them to the car. She placed them inside the trunk and hurried back inside to grab her sewing machine and supplies.

The two men, who were following her, were sitting and observing her from two houses away. They phoned Mitch to report what they saw.

"What do you mean she is taking things out of the apartment? Where is she going?"

"Evidently she is not staying with him and moving out."

"Follow her and find out where she lives," Mitch ordered and hung up abruptly.

"Okay boss," one man responded afterward.

The second car with the other men who were also sitting outside the apartment called in to Mitch and reported the same thing about Nate's wife. "It doesn't look like Nate is home. His wife is moving things out of the apartment. What do you want us to do now?"

"Stay there until he gets home. Let me know when that happens."

"Yes, boss." The men sat back and relaxed. It could be a while.

Maggie locked up the apartment and drove back to the YWCA with a full trunk. She took everything she could carry on the first trip and went back again for the rest. The car was only a day rental and was to be picked up later that day.

She didn't notice the car that was following her or the other car sitting outside of Nate's apartment. She was too involved in sorting out what her next move would be. When she arrived back at the YWCA, she rang the bell for some help. Her hands were full.

The clerk who was at the desk was new. She opened the door once Maggie identified herself and grabbed a bag out of Maggie's hand to assist her.

"Boy, you have a lot of laundry here, Mrs. Preston. Do you need help getting it to your room?"

"No, I can make a couple of trips with my friend's help. Thank you though."

Maggie put the bags and the sewing machine and supplies down near the stairs and called up to Branyrd to let her know she was back and needed a hand. The elevator was still out of order.

"Branyrd, can you come downstairs? I need some help getting this stuff up to my room."

"Sure, I'll be right there, Maggie."

Annie raced downstairs to help her mother too. "Wow, Mommy! What do you have in those bags? Are they more presents for me?"

"Sorry, honey. No, this is just our clothes and your toys and books. I thought you might like them."

"Thank you, Mommy. I missed my books. Now I'll be able to read at bedtime to Leana. She will love all my books, especially, *Louey the Lazy Elephant*. That's my favorite!"

Branyrd chuckled as she watched Annie look inside the bag and pull out her books and hurry back upstairs.

"Let me help you, Maggie. Give me the sewing machine and supplies. I'll be back for the other bag of Annie's things. You can't carry both bags up three flights of stairs."

"I know. I didn't realize how heavy clothes and toys would be," she sighed as she dragged the larger bag up the stairs.

After the final trip, Maggie tried to fit all the clothes into the small closet and the rest into the drawers.

"If you don't have room, you can put some stuff into my closet. I don't have much in there," Branyrd announced.

"Really? Thank you, Branyrd. I may take you up on that. I can put Annie's stuff in there, if you don't mind."

"Sure. I am only using one drawer. Annie can use the other three. There's plenty of room. There is nearly an empty closet too." Branyrd sent a message to Benedicto to empty the drawers and closet to make room for Annie's clothes.

He replied, "All done. I put all your stuff into the top drawer and also emptied the closet. If and when you need something I will send it along to you. No problem."

"Thank you, Benedicto," Branyrd replied in her head.

"Okay," Maggie sighed, feeling worn out.

"Listen, Maggie. Let me finish up unpacking this stuff in my room. You rest. You look exhausted. Annie can help me," Branyrd added.

"Yeah, Mommy. Let Branyrd and me do the rest. We are not tired, right, Branyrd?"

"That's right, Annie. We are not tired and can handle this. Let's get your things put away, Annie. Then we can go downstairs for a snack and Mommy can have some dinner before the kitchen closes."

"I already had dinner at Tracy's, Branyrd. But I could use a cup of coffee while Annie has her snack."

"Okay. Sounds good, Maggie. I will join you for a coffee in a little while."

Branyrd and Annie made quick work out of putting the clothes away and went back to get Maggie to join them in the dining room.

"I'm going to have some chocolate chip cookies. I could smell them when I came downstairs before, Branyrd. Do you want some too?" Annie asked with a wide smile.

"Maybe I'll try one. I never had any before," Branyrd said.

"What? You never had chocolate chip cookies before, Branyrd?" Annie asked with a shocked expression, too cute to ignore.

Branyrd and Maggie laughed at Annie's expression and followed her downstairs.

Benedicto spoke to Branyrd as she was sitting sampling a cookie with Annie who had two in each hand. He explained to the angel that someone was watching the YWCA and also Nate's apartment.

Branyrd spoke back to him in her mind as she nibbled and made smacking sounds over the delicious taste of chocolate in each cookie. She said she would keep a lookout on the street for anyone hanging around suspiciously.

Maggie sat beside Branyrd and asked, "You look a million miles away, Branyrd. Are you okay?"

"Oh, yes. Just enjoying my first chocolate chip cookie. These are delicious. I never realized how much I would love chocolate."

Annie smiled when she heard Branyrd's remark. "I told you that you would love them just like me!" she giggled and stuffed a second cookie into her overflowing mouth.

Maggie sipped her coffee, rolled her eyes at Annie and laughed along with her, unaware of the impending danger ahead.

CHAPTER TWENTY-NINE

Nate headed home after his latest interview for a job as a feed supply warehouse janitor and watchman. He had been hired on the spot. Nate had finally procured a job that would help him save some money to get his life back together.

As he pulled closer to his apartment he noticed a dark sedan, the same one that had been following him the other day sitting two houses away on his street. He decided to turn around instead and head in the opposite direction.

He suspected it was Mitch and the Gang keeping watch over him. They would not be satisfied until he paid them the cash he owed. He decided to pay Mitch a visit to the place where he last saw the White Stag Gang to give him back the drugs and call them even.

Nate stopped at the door of the ramshackle warehouse which was home to the White Stag Gang. They had used this warehouse for as long as Nate could remember under cover of a car dealership.

Mitch was quick to answer Nate's knock, looking none too pleased to see him. "What are you doing here?"

"Well, I figured you were looking for me with your henchmen parked outside my apartment. Here I am. I think we have to discuss matters once and for all, Mitch."

"We've already had a discussion, Nate. You know what you need to do – get me the money now!"

"I don't have the money and never will. I will not be selling drugs for you anymore, Mitch." Nate tossed the bag with the drugs that he had in his hand by the feet of the drug dealer and prepared to leave.

"Wait a minute, Nate! Where do you think you're going?"

"We are even now, Mitch. These are the drugs that I didn't sell. If you sell them, you will have the money you needed from me. Red Cap didn't come through with the money."

"It's not that simple, Nate. You owe me your time and money. But I will take the drugs back though. You still need to get me what you owe me."

"I don't owe you anything else, Mitch. Let me go. I am not going to do what you want. Find yourself another flunky!"

Nate turned his back on Mitch but stopped when he heard a gun being cocked. He next felt the tip of the gun at the back of his head.

"We are not finished here, Nate. You will do what I say and work for me for as long as I need you. If you do not do this then I will have to hurt someone you care about – like your daughter or wife."

Nate was at a loss for words as he turned around and faced Mitch and the gun he wielded in his hand.

***

Mitch's men grew tired of waiting outside Nate's house for hours and headed back to the warehouse when Mitch didn't answer his phone.

As they pulled into the driveway of the warehouse, they heard two gunshots and jumped out of the car to investigate with their own guns drawn.

They moved stealthily around the warehouse to the back and side doors. One man opened the side door and entered the building while the other man went to the back entrance. They moved around in the dark room keeping close to the walls and feeling their way around. A door slammed shut behind them.

"Someone just left." They looked through the darkness and turned on the flashlights of their phones.

"Whoever it was is gone now. Where's Mitch?"

They heard another noise and whispered as they got closer together, "Did you hear that? It sounds like someone is hurt."

One man ventured to call out, "Mitch, where are you?"

A groan was heard as they got further into the space and a body could be seen lying there covered in blood. They bent down to see who it was.

"We have to get out of here. Whoever did this will be back. I'll call an ambulance. There is nothing we can do for him now."

CHAPTER THIRTY

The two men who were sitting outside the YWCA keeping a watch for Nate's wife to come out, were jolted out of a nap by the ringing of their phones.

"Who is this?" one man answered but didn't recognize the number.

The man asked, "Mitch, is that you?"

There was no answer on either of their phones, just silence. They pulled out of the street and headed back to the warehouse. Something wasn't right.

"Who was that?" one man inquired.

"I have no idea. Who would be calling us on these phones? The phones were only for Mitch to use to connect to us.

Maybe something happened. Where are the other men? They were supposed to be watching Nate's house. Maybe they called us."

"It could be but I doubt it. Why would they call us? We were supposed to wait for Mitch to tell us what to do next. There's been no sign of Nate's wife leaving the YWCA."

"Well, I think we should go back and see what Mitch wants us to do. We can tell him about these strange phone calls too. Who else would have this number?"

"Good question, Mack. I have no idea. But something tells me we will soon find out."

They were quiet on the way back to the warehouse. As they turned the corner to turn into the driveway, they heard sirens and saw police cars pulling in beside them.

"What's going on, Mack? Why are the police here? We better get out of the way and fast. We don't want to be connected to whatever happened here."

Before the men could back up, the police were upon them blocking their way with guns out.

The two men were forced out of the car and told, "Hands up! Don't try anything!"

The men, wide-eyed and frightened did as they were told. They were quickly disarmed and escorted to a waiting police car. The two men watched an ambulance arrive and enter the building. A short time later a body was pulled out and put into the ambulance. The driver sped off in a hurry.

The men exchanged wary looks and took deep breaths. They kept watch to see who else came out of the building. No one did.

The police cordoned off the building with tape and one officer was left behind to protect the scene while the other car with the two men went to the station.

***

Benedicto watched the scene play out with Nate and Mitch. He knew that Mitch was going to kill Nate or worse, go after Annie and Maggie. He warned Branyrd. "Keep Annie and Maggie inside. There have been some new developments."

Branyrd excused herself from the dining room where she sat drinking coffee with Maggie and returned to her room so she could converse with Benedicto. She didn't like the sound of his voice and something about new developments. What did that mean?

When she entered her room Benedicto appeared in front of her and looked worried. She had never seen him like that.

"What happened, Benedicto?"

"Well, I didn't want to interfere but I had no choice."

"What did you do?"

He explained, "I followed Nate to the warehouse where the White Stag Gang housed their operation. I watched from the ceiling as the Gang leader, Mitch, held a gun to Nate's head. He was threatening him. He mentioned that Nate had to work for him or he would harm Maggie and Annie."

"Oh no! That can't happen, Benedicto! You have to do something," Branyrd cried out in alarm as she shook all over.

186

"I did what I could to stop Mitch. But…"

"What happened, Benedicto?"

***

Meanwhile Maggie and Annie knocked on Branyrd's door. "Branyrd, are you awake? Sorry to bother you. Just want to say, 'goodnight.'"

Branyrd opened the door and tried to act calm like nothing had happened and said, "Good night. Sleep well. See you in the morning."

She closed her door and sighed heavily as she leaned against the door and looked at Benedicto.

"What's going to happen now, Benedicto? What can we do?"

"HE will tell us. We must wait."

Branyrd sighed and lay down on her bed. She closed her eyes and looked up to Heaven for answers.

CHAPTER THIRTY-ONE

Back at the police station the two men were separated and taken to adjoining interrogation rooms. The two police officers who brought them in began the individual interrogations.

The man stared at the officer with frightened eyes and ventured to ask, "What did I do? Why am I here?"

"You are not the one asking questions. What is your name and why were you at the warehouse."

"My name is Mack Devers. I work for the car company who is in the warehouse."

"What do you do for this car company?"

"Well, I…um…" Mack began to sweat.

"Well, don't you know what your job is there?" the officer asked, demonstrating his impatience.

"I...um...drive cars to and from the people who purchase or sell them," Mack responded as he made up this position to cover himself. He relaxed a little and smiled.

"Why did you try to drive away when you saw us?" The officer leaned closer to intimidate Mack.

Mack cleared his throat and stuttered, "I was...um...I was returning after picking up a car."

"You didn't answer my question. Why did you try to run off?"

"What's going on? Why were the police at the warehouse? Who was hurt?"

"No questions. Sit here. I'll be back."

The officer went next door to see what the other man said during his interrogation. He sat next to his fellow officer who asked the second man the same questions.

"What is your name? Why were you at this warehouse?"

The second man was sweating profusely and wiped his brow on his shirt. "My name is Trent Carver. I was...I work for the operator of the car dealer who rents the warehouse."

"What do you do for this person?"

"Umm...I...I...drive around and do errands for him."

"Errands? What kind of errands do you do?"

"I...er...do whatever he needs me to do."

"Oh, I see. So, you pick up milk and bread and such for him?" the two officers chuckled at their humor.

Trent bent his head and didn't look at the officers. He was afraid that they would see the fear in his eyes. He knew he was in trouble.

The two officers got up abruptly and left the room without another word.

While Trent was sweating it out in one room, Mack was doing the same thing in another.

Mack's cell began to ring and so did Trent's.

The police had left their cell phones in the men's pockets on purpose, hoping to get a lead on the rest of the White Stag Gang.

CHAPTER THIRTY-TWO

Branyrd paced her small room and couldn't lay down. She was too wired to try to relax. What Benedicto had just told her left her shaken. What was going to happen next? Could she do anything to help?

She spoke out loud to HIM, "Can you help us, LORD? We need YOUR help desperately." Branyrd listened and waited for a response. She sighed and sat on her bed and clasped her hands in prayer. Something had to be done.

Branyrd couldn't tell Maggie and Annie. She didn't want them to worry. But she had to do something. Benedicto had told her to wait until HE told them what to do. She was too nervous to wait. She jumped off her bed and called out, "Benedicto, where are you?"

The Guardian Angel appeared, looking disheveled.

"What happened to you? You look like a wreck?"

Benedicto waved his hands over himself and cleaned up his appearance. "I was searching for Nate without using my powers. It's not as easy as it looks to find someone without HIS help. HE told me not to do anything but I was concerned about Nate's safety."

"Well, so am I, Benedicto! I haven't been able to lay down and relax enough to sleep. What are we going to do? I have prayed and called out to HIM but HE hasn't answered."

"I know. HE has plans for all of us. We have to sit tight. I know how hard it is for you to keep still, little angel. But still, you must stay, for a little while longer anyway. HE will let us know what to do."

"What do we say to Maggie and Annie? They will hear that something went wrong at the warehouse. Maggie knows Nate did work for the White Stag Gang leader who worked out of the warehouse. I don't want to frighten her. We need to know where he is."

"Yes, the two men who came to the warehouse are in police custody. They were outside when the police arrived. I don't know what they will say about why they were there. I'm sure they will go to prison as soon as what they were doing is uncovered."

"Well, they deserve to go there. They were the ones who beat up Nate. They could have killed him. But now…we don't know if Nate is all right."

"We do know that he is not in the hospital. He managed to escape after the gun went off in the struggle. The leader of the White Stag Gang may not live. He was gravely injured in the struggle. But if Mitch becomes lucid, he will tell the police who shot him. Nate could be in trouble then."

"Did you have something to do with that struggle, Benedicto?"

"Well, I did move the gun a little away from Nate or he would have been killed immediately. HE was not happy with my interference. HE said it was time for Nate to go but not for Mitch. Now HE said HE will take care of things and that we need to wait until HE summons us to move forward."

"Was HE angry with you, Benedicto?"

"Yes, HE was. I thought HE would burn me up with HIS eyes. They were terrifying to look at. I couldn't look away. HE wouldn't let me."

"Oh shit! Oops! Sorry about that! I know what they look like. HE has looked at me that way too! It was frightening and not something I will ever forget." Branyrd shivered at the thought.

"Don't worry, Branyrd. HE will let us know soon. Rest for now. I will keep a lookout in the meantime for Nate. If I see him, I can't do anything further to interfere with what HE has planned."

"Okay. I understand. It will be time to get up in a few hours anyway. I'll sit tight. Please let me know if you hear anything from HIM. I'm sure HE will answer you before HE answers me."

"Don't be too sure of that, Branyrd. I think HE is quite pleased with what you have done on your mission so far. But don't tell HIM I told you," Benedicto laughed as he disappeared into thin air.

Branyrd lay down on her bed and fell asleep. She didn't stir until she heard a knock on her door.

She got up and jumped into fresh clothes before answering the door.

Standing there was Annie with a bright sunny smile on her adorable face. "Hi Branyrd. Do you want to go down to breakfast with me and mommy? Mommy said it was okay to knock on your door since it wasn't too early this time. I waited an hour before I came over. Mommy said you might still be sleeping when the little hand was on the six and the big hand was on the 12. Were you?"

"Well, yes, I was, Annie. But now I am awake and ready to go downstairs for my morning cup of coffee."

"Mommy said she would be right down. She has to use the bathroom. You know…"

"Hmm, I see. Yes, I understand, Annie." Branyrd tried not to giggle at Annie's remark.

When they got downstairs the TV was on the latest news about a man who was injured in a warehouse.

Branyrd led Annie away from the TV and diverted her attention to the food being set out for breakfast. She could feel her stomach turning over at the scents of bacon, sausage, eggs and pancakes. She knew she would never eat any of that. Annie, on the other hand, was loading up her plate as usual.

Branyrd marveled at what this little girl could eat. She wondered how she put it away.

A short time later Maggie joined them at the table and settled in with toast and coffee. She had stopped by previously to watch the news and relayed what she had heard to Branyrd.

"There was a man injured in a warehouse last night, Branyrd. Do you think it could be Nate?" she whispered so Annie couldn't hear.

"What makes you think it could be Nate? What would he be doing in a warehouse at night?"

"Well, I know he would go there to see Mitch, the man he used to work for. He was the one who beat Nate up for not paying him back. What if it was Nate who got injured."

"Well, I don't know. I'm sure you would have been informed by the police or the hospital by now and heard if he was injured, Maggie."

"But what if he didn't have any identification on him? How would the police or hospital know to call me?"

"Well, I think the police always find a way to get next of kin in the case of an injured person."

"Do you think so, Branyrd? I hope so. I will keep my cell with me and on vibrate and ring just in case. It's funny that I haven't heard from him since he gave Annie the doll for her birthday. I thought he would try to contact us again. He seemed to be trying to change."

"Yes, I think he did seem better than before. Maybe he is busy today and can't get to a phone. Wasn't he going to look for a job?"

"Look for a job? Who told you that, Branyrd? Did Nate tell you that?"

"I...I thought you did, Maggie. I haven't spoken to Nate." Branyrd avoided meeting Maggie's eyes. She couldn't tell Maggie that she knew what Nate was doing in the warehouse. Benedicto had told her what Nate had said to Mitch before their struggle with the gun about obtaining a new job.

Branyrd had to be careful. She sighed and spoke to Benedicto in her head. "Where are you? Do you know anything yet?"

CHAPTER THIRTY-THREE

Trent and Mack answered their phones simultaneously in separate rooms.

"Where are you?" Mack asked.

Trent was asking his caller the same thing next door.

"We were at the warehouse and found Mitch in a pool of blood. Someone had shot him. We called for an ambulance and then got out of there as fast as we could. We didn't want to be blamed for his possible death. Do you know if he is still alive?"

"No. We saw a body being taken away. We don't know what happened. Did you see anyone around?"

"No. But we were in such a hurry to leave that we didn't look."

"We can't talk anymore now because the police may be listening to us. Talk to you later when we get out of here. Let's meet at our usual place. You know where I mean?"

"Do they have anything on you?"

"No. We are innocent. I'm going to call a lawyer to hurry things along. I'm sure we will get bailed out soon."

"Good to hear. We'll be waiting for you both."

Mack sighed and only hoped Trent hadn't said too much on his call to get them into any more trouble.

***

The police were listening in on both calls and smiled. They got them. They traced the calls and found the other two men.

Two cruisers headed over to the meeting place, Tracy's Diner, and picked up the unsuspecting men.

The officers went back into the interrogation rooms and pulled the men out. They were placed into jail cells until further information was needed. The officers had to make room for the two new suspects who were on their way there now.

Grumbling could be heard as the officers pulled the two new suspects into the separate interrogation rooms to begin their grilling.

The officers came out after two hours of cross-examination of the two men. The men admitted to being members of the White Stag Gang and that the man who was shot was their leader.

Celebrations were all around as the officers high-fived one another over being successful in capturing the men responsible for selling drugs that harmed so many young kids and others over the past several years.

The captain announced, "We have scored a big one today, people! We have been after the White Stag Gang for too long! Congratulations to all the officers involved in this case. We will put these men away for a long time. Also, the hospital called and said that Mitch is still not out of danger. The doctor said Mitch may not make it. If Mitch does make it though, we will question him about who shot him and then put Mitch away. Maybe we will go after the person who shot Mitch or not. Whoever he/she is, did us a favor by taking Mitch down," the captain laughed and shook each officer's hand.

CHAPTER THIRTY-FOUR

Benedicto summoned Branyrd. "Mitch is still not out of danger. Nate is still on the run. You and I will find Nate with HIS help. Excuse yourself from Maggie and Annie and meet me outside in front of the YWCA."

Branyrd nodded and turned to Maggie and Annie. "I'm kind of tired. I think I will take a nap. I didn't sleep well last night. Please excuse me. See you later."

"Okay, Branyrd, see later. Rest up." Maggie said.

"See you soon, Branyrd," Annie seconded with a smile. "Take a couple of cookies to bed with you. There are still some left."

"Thanks, Annie. I think I will. I might get hungry when I wake up," Branyrd smiled back at her and patted Annie on the head as she passed by.

Branyrd hurried up the stairs and then went out the back door at the end of the corridor to look for Benedicto.

He was standing out front looking like he hadn't a care in the world while she was shaking all over. He pulled her close to him and they flew through the air landing a mile away in the parking lot of an abandoned building.

"What are we doing here, Benedicto? And, why didn't you warn me about that flying thing? You scared me half to death. I can do that in Heaven but not here on Earth in this body," Branyrd said in exasperation.

"No worries, little angel. This was the fastest way to get us here. We can't waste time. The police will be on the lookout for the gun and the person who was responsible. It is all a matter of time before they connect Nate to Mitch's injury."

"Did HE tell you this and where to find Nate?"

"Well, of course HE did. How would I know where Nate was?"

Branyrd looked at Benedicto with a sly expression on her angelic face showing that she didn't believe a word he said.

"Where is Nate? I don't see him here."

"Come with me. He's hiding inside the building. Let's go get him."

"Wait! What are we going to do when we find him, Benedicto? What are we going to tell him?"

"HE will tell us. Don't worry, Branyrd. HE knows what HE is doing at all times even if we don't."

"Okay. Who am I to question HIM?" Branyrd followed Benedicto into the dark and decrepit building.

"You need to call out to Nate. If he knows it's you, he will not be frightened. If he sees me, he will run the other way. We did not get along well on our last meeting."

"What? He saw you? When was that?" Branyrd asked in mock surprise. "I heard about that," Branyrd tittered.

"Never mind that. Just call out to him. We can't waste time. The police will be here soon."

Branyrd shrugged her shoulders and called out, "Nate. Where are you? It's Branyrd, Maggie's friend."

Nate came out of his hiding place. "Branyrd? What are you doing here?"

"I can't tell you that now. You must hurry. You have to come with us."

"Us? Who else is here?" Nate looked around anxiously.

"Just do as I say. Okay. I'll bring you to Maggie and Annie. They are both worried about you. They haven't heard from you since you dropped off Annie's present."

"I know. I've been kind of busy."

"Yes, I can see you were."

"How do you know what I was doing?"

"I didn't say I did. All I know is you must come with me now."

In the distance a few sirens could be heard as Nate followed Branyrd out the back way and into the arms of Benedicto.

"Do the police know I'm here?" Looking shocked when he spotted Benedicto he said, "Why is he here?"

"No questions, Nate. I am your ride. Hold on tight. It may be a little bumpy."

"Whoa, wait a minute! What's happening here?" Nate exclaimed as he looked around in vain for a vehicle.

Benedicto took hold of both Branyrd and Nate in his arms as he flew them back to the YWCA and safety. When they arrived, Branyrd got them inside through a locked back door with the help of Benedicto's magic. Branyrd and Nate went up to Maggie and Annie's room. Benedicto disappeared from view after completing the LORD's instructions.

Nate took a deep breath and said to Branyrd, "What just happened? Things keep getting weirder and weirder all the time! Can you please explain what's going on?"

"Everything will be all right. Don't worry, Nate. You can stay here with Maggie and Annie until it is safe for you to go back to your apartment."

"What do you mean? Are the police looking for me? Do they know I killed Mitch? It was an accident!"

"Well, Mitch did not die. He was brought to the hospital and is unconscious so the police don't know who shot him yet. We know it was an accident. All will be taken care of. Please do not worry. You must stay inside while you are here. The clerk would eject you if she knew you were here," Branyrd explained.

"Mitch is…not dead? Thank God. I thought I was going back to prison for life this time. But when he wakes up, he will tell them I shot him. Won't he?"

"No, we will make sure he doesn't remember what happened," Branyrd continued.

"What do you mean you will make sure he doesn't remember?"

"What you need to do now, Nate, is not worry about anything. You are in good hands. You should be with your family. Make amends and get back to your lives together. Your daughter and wife need you," Branyrd instructed.

Branyrd waved her hand over Nate as instructed by HIM and Nate calmed right down. Nate sighed and looked at Branyrd with a confused expression. All he could do was nod to Branyrd and follow her instructions especially after seeing the man in the background looking at him. The same man who flew him through the air, had visited him at his apartment and given him a warning about getting his act together. This man looked a lot smaller and less imposing than previously. Maybe he imagined the man being so large before. *But how did he fly? I must be losing my mind,* Nate mused.

Branyrd noticed the look of surprise on Nate's face when he spotted Benedicto in the background.

"Are you okay, Nate?"

"I guess so. I am still trying to process what just happened. Did I imagine it all?" Nate asked in confusion.

"No, but it is not going to stay with you very long."

"What? Now I am really confused," Nate sighed heavily.

"It's okay," Branyrd said and smiled to put Nate at ease as she waved her hands as instructed by HIM over Nate's forehead erasing the flight from his mind. He had enough to deal with all the other stuff that was already there.

Branyrd smiled and nodded at her Guardian Angel and waited by Nate's side as he knocked on his wife's door. It took a few minutes before Maggie opened the door in shock when she saw Nate.

"What are you doing here, Nate? How did you get in?"

Branyrd stepped into view and responded for Nate, "I found him with the help of my friend. He needs to be here with you until things cool down."

"What things, Branyrd? What are you talking about?"

"I will explain everything to you, Maggie," Branyrd replied.

"Oh my God! You mean he had something to do with that man who was shot at the warehouse?"

Maggie's raised voice woke up Annie as she came to the door and looked out. "Daddy! You came here to see us? Come in and see our room." She pulled her father by the hand around her mother and told him to sit on her bed.

Branyrd smiled at Maggie and shrugged her shoulders. "Come to my room. I don't want Annie to hear this. I have a lot to tell you."

Once they were settled in Branyrd's room, the angel began to tell Maggie about how her friend was responsible for rescuing Nate after the accident at the warehouse. Of course, leaving out the fact that both she and her friend were angels.

Maggie gasped and tears filled her eyes. "Will Nate have to go to prison for what he did?"

"No, my friend will get a lawyer for Nate if needed and all will be taken care of quickly. Mitch will not remember who shot him. Don't worry, Maggie. Just take care of your family. That is all that matters.

"How do you know that Mitch will not remember anything?" Maggie's voice shook.

"I don't think that Mitch will make it to remember. I told you anything is possible when you pray to HIM. Right, Maggie?"

"Oh, Branyrd! You prayed for this to happen to help us? Did you do all this?" Maggie raised her brows as she waited for Branyrd to answer.

"No, I didn't do anything, Maggie. Only GOD knows what will happen. Just believe in him, pray and be as good a person as you are now."

Maggie smiled, embraced Branyrd and hurried back to her room to see her husband and daughter.

Branyrd felt tears forming in her eyes as she watched Maggie leave. She knew it would be the last time she would see her. She turned to see Benedicto standing there waiting for her.

"Can I just see them one more time?" Branyrd begged with tears brimming.

Benedicto picked up the feather-weight angel and flew her into Maggie's room where they hovered at the ceiling to watch the happy reunion of the family. The family was unaware of their presence.

Annie was excited to have her father there and couldn't stop jabbering about anything and everything she had done since she last saw him. Her precious doll was in her arms the whole time.

Maggie held tightly to Nate's hand as he stroked his thumb up and down her hand. Branyrd could see how much they loved each other.

"Will they be okay now, Benedicto? Is there anything else I can do to make sure they are safe?"

"No, HE said HE would make sure all will be forgotten about Nate and that the family will return to their apartment and get on with their lives once again as if nothing happened. Mitch will be joining HIM at the Gate shortly but not allowed to enter. GOD has another place reserved just for Mitch."

"Oh my! I bet HE does. Does that mean that Maggie and Annie will forget me?"

"Hmm. I'm sorry, little angel. That is the way it has to be."

"But won't they remember anything?" Branyrd beseeched her Guardian Angel to answer positively.

"No. But don't worry. There will be more missions and others for you to help. This is only the beginning, Branyrd. You have much to do in the near future. Just remember how good it felt to help others and do HIS bidding."

Branyrd sighed heavily and said, "I guess so. But I will miss Maggie and Annie so much. They have become precious to me."

"I know, Branyrd. I know." Benedicto looked up and smiled.

"What? You know something, Benedicto, don't you? Did HE just talk to you now?" Branyrd's eyes were pleading.

"HE said that maybe they would remember a little about a special friend they had while they lived at the YWCA."

"Really? Oh, hot damn! Oops, I mean holy moly!"

A titter could be heard reverberating around them as Benedicto and Branyrd flew back to Heaven.

CHAPTER THIRTY-FIVE

HEAVEN

Branyrd watched from above the happy reunion of the family she had helped. The window was slowly closing and she kept her eyes on the three of them as they moved back into the little apartment.

She smiled and nodded in contentment as the window was closed completely by the LORD's hand.

"Thank you, LORD, for letting me see them one more time. They look so happy. They are safe now, aren't they?"

"Yes, they are, Branyrd. They have you to thank for all you did to make this possible."

"But I really didn't do anything, LORD. Benedicto helped make all this possible."

"What you forget is that I see all and know all, Branyrd. I saw how you orchestrated the mission in your own inimitable way. Good job, Angel First Class!"

"Thank you, LORD! I…I…only did what you requested of me, LORD. I really didn't do anything special."

"Ahh, but you are special, Branyrd. That is why I chose you to do this mission and the next."

"Did you say the next, LORD? Am I going to go on another mission?" Branyrd exclaimed excitedly, her face breaking into a wide smile.

"Yes, I have a special one just for you, Branyrd. Do you think you can handle it?

"Oh, hot da….! Oops! I mean holy mackerel! I definitely can handle anything you give me, LORD!" Branyrd averted her eyes, after she had dropped another zinger, in fear of being burned by HIS lightning-lit eyes.

When she looked up again HE was no longer above her but she could hear HIS distinctive titter as it echoed and slowly faded away.

Watch for more missions for Branyrd the Angel in upcoming books.

ABOUT THE AUTHOR

Janice Spina is a retired administrative secretary from a public school system in Massachusetts. She has always loved writing poetry, novels and children's stories. She published her first book in 2013 and hasn't stopped since.

This is the 40th book Janice has published. She also has two mystery series of six books each, one for boys and the other for girls even though they are enjoyed by both boys and girls. She has a fantasy series of two books with more to come for YA.

Janice has published 19 children's stories for young children. She also writes under J.E. Spina and has published five novels and a short story collection for 18+.

She can be reached at these links.

Website: http://Jemsbooks.com
Blog: https://Jemsbooks.blog
Twitter: http://twitter.com/janice_spina
FB Main Page: http://facebook.com/janice.spina.9
FB Author Page: http://facebook.com/janicespina7
FB Novelist Page: http://facebook.com/jespina7

Janice lives in New Hampshire with her husband, John, and two tanks of fish. John is the illustrator of her children's books and designer of all her book covers.

If you enjoyed this book, please leave a review where you purchased it and spread the word to your family and friends.

Janice loves to hear from readers and welcomes reviews from wherever her books are purchased. She says, 'It's like Christmas each time I receive a review!'

If you would like to be on Janice Spina's email list to receive updates, newsletters, and special deals on books, please follow her at her blog/website above.

Watch for more books coming from Jemsbooks.

A NOTE FROM THE AUTHOR

This is the first book in this series about an angel. I infused some comedy into this sometimes-serious story. It deals with many issues that are evident in our world today. I hope you will find it entertaining.

This series is written for young adults – Ages 18+. I hope you enjoyed this work of fiction. Watch for more books in this series coming over the new few years.

Thank you for purchasing one of Jemsbooks. I appreciate your kind support of me and my books. If you like this book, a review would be greatly appreciated wherever you purchased it. Reviews and word of mouth are the best way to spread your thoughts about books. Please share your review with friends and family. I would love to hear from you. You can reach me at jjspina(@comcast.net.

All my books are available on Amazon and Barnes & Noble. Watch for more books coming for all ages.

With Blessings & Love,

Janice Spina

OTHER MG/PT/YA BOOKS BY JANICE SPINA

Davey & Derek Junior Detectives Book 1:
The Case of the Missing Cell Phone
  (Pinnacle Book Achievement Award,
  Honorable Mention- Readers' Favorite Book
Award)

Davey & Derek Junior Detectives Book 2:
The Case of the Mysterious Black Cat
  (Pinnacle Book Achievement Award)

Davey & Derek Junior Detectives Book 3: The
Case of the Magical Ivory Elephant
  (Pinnacle Book Achievement Award & Reader's
  Favorite Book Awards – Silver Medal)

Davey & Derek Junior Detectives Book 4: The
Case of the Brown Scraggly Dog
  (Top Shelf Book Awards – First Place
  Finalist in Red City Review Awards & 5-Star
Book Review – Readers' Favorite Book Awards)

Davey & Derek Junior Detectives Book 5:
The Case of the Sad Mischievous Ghost
(Pinnacle Book Achievement Award &
Authorsdb
Cover Contest – Silver Medal)

Davey & Derek Junior Detectives Book 6: The
Case of the Mystery of the Bells
(Pinnacle Book Achievement Award, Finalist –
Readers' Favorite Book Awards, Finalist – Book
Excellence Awards)

Abby & Holly School Dance
(Pinnacle Book Achievement Award & Bronze
Medal from Readers' Favorite Book Awards)

Abby & Holly Series Book 2: Unfortunate Events
(Pinnacle Book Achievement Award, Readers'
Favorite Book Awards – Honorable Mention)

Abby & Holly Series, Book 3, Secrets of the
Trunk
(Pinnacle Book Achievement Award)

Abby & Holly Series, Book 4, The Hidden
Stairway

(Pinnacle Book Achievement Award)

Abby & Holly Series, Book 5, The Copper Key
(Pinnacle Book Achievement Award)

Abby & Holly Series, Book 6, Faulty Timeline
(Pinnacle Book Achievement Award)

YA BOOKS BY JANICE SPINA

The Legend of the Taken Ones (Gateskin Chronicles Book 1)

(5-Star Review from Readers' Favorite Book Awards)

The Unknown Territory (Gateskin Chronicles Book 2)

BOOKS BY J.E. SPINA FOR 18+

Hunting Mariah

(Finalist in Authorsdb First Lines Contest)

Mariah's Revenge

(Finalist in Authorsdb First Lines Contest)

How Far is Heaven

An Angel Among Us: A Short Story Collection

In A Second

Lubelia Alycea: One Hundred Years

www.ingramcontent.com/pod-product-compliance
Lightning Source LLC
Chambersburg PA
CBHW070756280626
47162CB00016B/1069